The Argentum Lupus: Book One of the Alpha Chronicles

By

Roderick Chapman

Dedication

To my parents, for their unwavering support and guidance.
To Brittany, my love and my rock, thank you for your endless
encouragement and for always believing in me.
And to my children—Desiree, Kyler, Cheyanna, Liana, Charlotte,
and Nicky—you are my greatest inspiration and the driving force
behind everything I do.
This is for all of you.

"Power is not a means, it is an end. One does not establish a dictatorship in order to safeguard a revolution; one makes the revolution in order to establish the dictatorship."

-George Orwell

Table of Contents

[Chapter 1] — The Mark

The sun was blinding as ever today. He lifted his arm and shielded his eyes to see the clouds in the sky; it was for nought as there wasn't a cloud to be seen. A sweltering summer day was just ramping up. As he lowered his hand, he saw a pretty 20-something-year-old brunette girl with far too much make-up on, smiling at him.

An average man, Luther Hyde was never one to turn heads though neither was he unaccustomed to getting the occasional pretty smile from a passing tourist. He smiled in return but continued on his way. She was cute, but his ledger was full today, and he was not able to loiter and flirt. Probably only wanted the vacation fling, at any rate. The facts, mind you these were solely in his head facts, were enough to tell him that it would have been a waste of time. He did this frequently as he believed he lacked the proper attributes to successfully woo the tens of thousands of tourists who visited Bermuda every year. He simply wasn't "exotic" enough to garner true attention. And at 37, he had quit attempting to gain their favour.

His primary focus was on getting back to Berkley Institute to grade the tests before his lunch was completely exhausted. He mounted his bike near the moon gate at the Spanish Point boat club, started it and sped off towards the high school.

A scooter had been hit by a tourist driving one of the new electric four-wheelers at the intersection of Spanish Point Road and North Shore Road, so he had to take St John's Road to get back, and the delay cost him the remaining time for lunch. He shrugged; nothing he could do but grade the tests after school now. He was just disheartened as he knew the kids were turning in their reports on St George today, and he had promised to get them back to them the next day. Late night tonight, simply couldn't be helped as he was not about to go back on his word for any reason.

The rest of the school day went by as the usual school day. There was, unfortunately, a fight that broke out outside of his classroom. Someone made the wrong "yo mama" joke today and got busted in his lip for it. It took him nearly two minutes to reach the two pugilists and then even longer to separate them. He reached them not a moment too soon, however, as one had the other's tie and was pulling it tightly around his quarrel's neck. Hyde managed to pull them apart and slipped the bluing teen's tie away from their throat before things really got out of hand. He threatened the onlookers and instigators with detention, and they dispersed rapidly enough to satisfy him. He then led the two angry boys down to the principal's office, who, of course, was not there yet as she was in a meeting. He sat the boys down and attempted to ask the secretary if he would watch them but was promptly shot down as the man was grabbing his things to run and pick his own children up from their primary school.

It was a long two hours before Ms Lee made it back from her meeting, and by the time he had both boys explain the situation from their sides, added what he witnessed and assisted with punishments, it was well after 6:30 in the evening. Once he returned to his classroom and completed the grading he wanted to get done, it was pushing 10 p.m. Stretching and simultaneously groaning at the time, he packed up and headed out to the deserted parking lot where he had parked his bike. As he was in the trunk, pulling out his helmet and stowing his briefcase, he heard what sounded like a muffled scream from the football field behind him. He froze and listened to see if the sound might have been just his imagination. The silence was odd because not even the frogs and toads were singing. Nevertheless, he shook the thought and turned back to what he was doing. He had just latched the trunk when the sound of a choked gurgling reached his ears this time.

Well, never one to not help, he turned and walked towards the trees that separated the high school from Dandy Town Hornets' football field. When he made it to the edge of cedars and rubber trees, he pulled up short. He wanted to help, but it was black as pitch, and those trees could easily snap his ankle if he wasn't careful. He damned his caution and stepped in, however, moving carefully and feeling his way along. As he neared the other side of the tree line, the moon came out and bathed the area in cool moonlight, exposing the sad sight before him…

Lying about a hundred feet out, a body was badly maimed and unmoving. From the gold and green of the person's clothing, he knew this was one of the students of Berkley dead or dying before him. He knew the gym uniform well. With the knowledge that it might even be one of his own students, he rushed out to the poor… person. Gender was impossible to determine, not only thanks to the lack of proper lighting but also because the remains were far too non-descript to properly identify. In fact, they almost looked like… non-human remains mixed with shreds of the gym uniform.

There was a twig that snapped off to his right, and he snapped his head in that direction. Clouds, the same fucking clouds that had been so absent during the day, now shrouded the area he needed to see in deep, impenetrable shadow. Realising that whatever had made the macabre scene he stumbled upon had created it as some gruesome trap, Hyde began slowly backing away towards the trees he had only moments ago fretted so much about. Now that he was exposed, they seemed like complete safety. He still did not take his eyes away from the area that the noise had come from, but the clouds continued to stymy his attempts to identify their origin.

Just as he was nearing the tree line and his imagined sanctuary, the clouds began to part, and bright moonlight flooded the area. What he saw defied any possible creatures and monsters that his mind filled the gap in information with. There, creating its own menacing shadow that eliminated any definable detail, was a larger-than-possible wolf? He wasn't sure, and his uncertainty caused him to hesitate and try to look harder to see if what he was seeing was what he was thinking it was. Logic rebelled at the notion that it was a wolf; there were no large predators on the island, for there was no way for them to get here, much less anything large enough for them to survive on, even if they had. As his idiotic mind sat there and pondered these ridiculous facts, another set of clouds flowed deep shadows over the field. The loss of sight on the… creature, he still wasn't willing to conclude "wolf",… caused him to focus better and realise that no matter what it was, he was in danger. Thankfully, this bank of clouds moved much faster than the last set and the area was flooded with moonlight again. His eyes desperately scanned the field, simultaneously praying to find this creature and praying not to. The field was empty now, aside from the bloody cause of his presence in this nightmare.

Without witnessing the unknown creature again so briefly after having "seen" it in the first place caused his logic centre to immediately discount the shadow-soaked visage to simply be the over-imaginative thinking of a man exhausted from a day's labour.

He turned away from the location of the apparition and stepped into the tree line. He once again stepped carefully to avoid twisting his ankle and resolved to call the police service to report the visceral scene in the field so they could investigate. There was some light rustling of leaves as he moved towards his scooter, and he unknowingly picked up his pace.

He saw the parking lot through the leaves, comfortingly flooded with artificial light from the streetlights and began to calm his racing heart. Clearly, he needed to stop watching those ridiculous horror movies he loved so much. They were causing his imagination to run a little too wild. He was stepping out to his salvation when the attack happened.

One moment, he was feeling relieved at the prospect of heading home to write on that forum he enjoyed so much about the bizarre situation he had found himself in and the next, he was hit with all the force of a truck, slamming him face down in the dirt just within the tree line. He tried to scream for help, but a deep, guttural growl made him just freeze. Within a breadth of a moment, however, his mind went into survival mode, and he lashed out behind him with a right elbow, connecting solidly with something hot and furry. He hammered his elbow into the attacker in hopes of inflicting enough trauma to avoid his own demise to this silent hunter. Instead, he found both of his arms pinned to the ground, and a searing hot sensation flared across his back as he realised whatever had him pinned had just bitten deeply into his flesh. Having always been a fighter, Hyde screamed and kicked with his legs, not afraid anymore but infuriated that he was pinned and unable to dole out an ounce of the damage his attacker was giving him. His feet did connect with the being that had him so secure but were largely ineffectual. His screaming proved to be his saving grace as a group of young men came running into the parking lot. At their incoming presence, the attacker left as quickly as he had appeared.

Spinning quickly to try and glean some details from the attacker, Hyde only saw a shadow melt into the gloom provided by the tree canopy. Shaken beyond anything he had felt before, he stumbled out of the trees into the paved parking lot just as his unwitting saviours reached him. They pulled him further from the trees, having seen he was, in fact, bleeding badly and, therefore, in need of help. Streams of unanswerable questions were hurled at him as one called for the police and an ambulance, but all Hyde could do was stare into the trees and wonder why he was alive. Clearly, the attacker possessed a strength surpassing his own, had plenty of time to end his feeble struggle before the boys came along, and had the means with his teeth to rip him to shreds… so, why was he still amongst the living and not just another gruesome crime scene?

Hyde woke in his hospital bed to the sounds of the nurse coming in and checking his vitals. The hospital room at King Edward VII Memorial Hospital was spacious, made necessary as the constables and chief inspector were constantly streaming in and out of his room in the two days since his attack. They wanted to know what happened.

Well, of course, they want to know what happened; he bloody well did, too! But he knew nothing. He told them all about the noises that drove him to the football field, to begin with, the gruesome display laid out for him to discover; he skipped the viewing of the "wolf" he had imagined (still refusing to believe it had been possible), then recounted the details of the attack itself. They were quite sceptical over the fact that Hyde was unable to fight off this would-be killer as he was average, but sturdy built, but they had no other choice than to accept his version of the story.

Throughout the whole retelling, retelling, and even more retelling of the bizarre story, the prevailing thoughts of why he was still breathing kept circling to the forefront of his mind. Even the chief inspector had asked that question, though he had intended to speak it in his mind rather than voicing it in front of the victim. After muttering a shameful apology, he made to leave but stopped short at the door and put another thought in Hyde's mind: "Why were you targeted like that? Do you have any enemies?"

Hyde admitted that aside from the minor tussle he had back in primary school, he did not really interact with anyone, much less get into any fights or altercations that would suggest a planned attack on him. But as the chief inspector wished him well and suggested calling him should any other details come to him, Hyde's mind began running over every interaction he could think of. Had he inadvertently made himself a mortal enemy somehow…? Nothing and no one sprung to mind immediately, but obviously, someone chose him for a reason.

As he pondered this possibility, he noticed a young-looking Latinx man looking at him through the open hospital door. It was only a glance, but the look in the boy's eyes looked… ancient? Is that the right word? It didn't seem possible that the boy, *maybe* 18, would be capable of having eyes that very much looked like they belonged to a much, much older man. He chalked it up to the trauma of the attack, causing him to see things again.

The doctor was talking to him, so he focused on what he was saying.

"…likely going to cause you to be in quite a bit of pain for the rest of your life," he was saying.

"I'm sorry, my mind was wandering. Could you repeat that?"

"Sure. I was saying that the damage to your shoulder muscles was extensive. Given the amount of damage and the fact that we had to pull muscles back together, you are likely going to deal with a lot of pain for the rest of your life. We will give you plenty of time to heal and then at least twelve months of physical therapy to know for sure, but this is a safe assumption given how extensive the tear is."

"Is there nothing more you can do? Reconstructive surgery or something?"

"If you would like us to attempt that, we will, but I will say that there is a large margin of error, unfortunately. But let's have a look at it and see how it looks as we swap out your bandages."

As the rubbery cloth bandages unwound from his back, the lack of physical discomfort startled him. He had taken a nasty spill on his bike a few years back and gave himself road rash on his right arm, still carried the scar, in fact, and whenever they changed the bandages, it felt as if they were reopening the wound with a hot knife. Oddly enough, this time, nothing.

As the bandage and blood-soaked gauze fell away, Hyde heard a shocked gasp from the doctor and nurse at the same time.

"What is it? Has it gotten infected or something?!" His alarmed tone mirrored the look in the doctor's eyes as he surveyed the wound.

"Not… exactly…" came the hesitant response.

No longer willing to be patient, Hyde leapt from the bed rushed over to the bathroom and twisted carefully in the mirror to assess the destruction of his shoulder for himself. Though he prepared himself for what he thought was anything, he ran his hand over the spot where the man had viciously mauled him, only to his astonishment, touched nothing but unblemished skin. Not even so much as a scar to remind him of his ordeal.

"That is… im-im-impossible!" was the alarmed assessment from the veteran doctor. "I saw you when you came in, and frankly, you were lucky to have saved your arm, much less this!"

Before Hyde could try to calm the man, two brown-skinned hands appeared on either side of the doctor's head and twisted until his neck popped grotesquely, and he went limp in the hands that ended his life. The killer let go, and the doctor dropped lifelessly to the floor and lay next to the similarly departed nurse. In the space where the doctor had stood was now the Latinx boy with the ancient eyes, eyes that now burned with silent rage.

"I had really hoped to have avoided that," he muttered in a heavy South American accent. "I was trying to get in here to talk to you before the doctor came in to check on the bandages but got hung up by the lady guarding the floor. Please forgive me for this *terrible necesidad*. My name is Bembe, and I am here to help you, Milord."

His manners and now deference towards him unsettled Hyde. This young man just killed two people and was now speaking to him as if he were some kind of royalty?!

Before he could say anything in return, there was a noise from outside the room, and Bembe turned in preparation for another necessary kill when Hyde launched himself out of the window and onto the narrow overhang outside. With skill he did not believe he possessed, he jumped up, twisted, and pulled himself to the roof in a fluid, graceful movement. He did not take the time to examine this latest information and simply sprinted to the fire escape, barely touching the metal steps before leaping the last 12 feet to the ground and ducking in the foliage near the hospital. There, he froze, waiting for signs of discovery or possible pursuit by the murderer he just escaped from. No shouts of alarm. He looked to the roof to see Bembe had made the roof and was silently scanning for him around the hospital grounds.

Grateful for the dense canopy offered by the sub-tropic trees of his home, he waited for Bembe to check the other side of the roof and then sprinted towards the Botanical Gardens to consider his next move. He skirted the Masterworks Museum and then used the foliage to, once again, disappear in the thick green vegetation. Going down into a hardly used sitting atrium area to gather his wits. He sat on the old bench and noted that he was not winded in the slightest but logged it as "not pressing" and began to contemplate his next move.

"Mr Hyde?" A man's voice came from the top of the stairs he had not used yet. For the seemingly thousandth time, he froze, not knowing whether or not he should answer. Shuffling on the stairs, he had used to get down here informed him that this man was not alone. Oddly comforting, considering the last stranger he had met seemed to be alone. He was about to answer when the thought occurred to him: what if he was mistaken and Bembe had an accomplice?

He was not given long enough to consider this when a man appeared on the curve of the stairs before him, dressed as a police constable. Hyde audibly sighed in relief. Definitely **not** Bembe.

"Uh, yes, constable. I am Luther Hyde. I am sorry for running from the scene, but a man killed two people, and I was afraid he would be after me next…" he trailed off, finally noting that this constable was not only **massive** but also… Samoan? That made no sense as there were no Samoans on the island that could be local enough to join the police service. Small islands tend to afford most locals this kind of information.

"It is okay," the large man said in what was likely supposed to be a soothing tone but came out more as a threat. "We found the man and have him secure, but we need you to come identify him."

An even bigger Black man walked down the stairs behind him. He looked Bermudian, at least. Not convinced these two were actually with the police service, but certain he was not able to defend against an attack by a not only numerical but physically superior force.

"Yeah… of course I will," he managed to say. Shockingly, both men visibly relaxed at the sound of his cooperation. Curious…

[Chapter 2] — The Turning

They walked to the police car that was sitting and waiting for them with another Black constable in the driver's seat. The Samoan held the door for him while the first Black constable got in the backseat on the far side. After Hyde had gotten in, the Samoan motioned for him to scoot in, which he did, though puzzled. The Samoan got in next to him, and no sooner did the door close than the car took off. The excitement of running from Bembe had made Hyde not realise that the day was almost over. As they traversed the cramped streets towards the North Shore, the shadows got longer by the minute it seemed. Realising that their trip was already longer than absolutely necessary, Hyde looked to the driver and asked, "I'm sorry, but I thought we were going to the scene of the crime, and that is back that way?"

"Our orders were to take you to the station at St David's," came a terse reply.

Expecting more information, but seeing the man refocus on the drive told him he was getting nothing more. He legitimately began to panic as this seemed highly irregular. Why send a witness to the station furthest from the crime scene? He looked at his "bodyguards" out of the corner of his eye and realised that he was not being treated as a witness but a suspect.

As they turned onto North Shore Road, the sun was beginning to sink below the waves, and Hyde's hope for making it out of his situation sank with it. His blood was pumping strong, and he noticed his hearing became noticeably sharper. Dismissed by his survival mode, this would prove to be his first redeeming quality. He heard a slight static, which he attributed to adrenalin-fuelled paranoia.

His concern never truly went away as time passed. Despite the island being so small, it would take them nearly an hour to get to St David's. While going through Flatt's, there was a tourist embroiled in a massive argument with another tourist as they both were attempting to pet the sea turtles at the aquarium, but some sort of dispute broke out, and when the fists began to fly, a crowd gathered and caused a stop in traffic.

None of the supposed "constables" seemed interested in helping to resolve the issue; in fact they studiously ignored it and continued to be as stoic as they had been the whole ride, which only compounded his worry. The increase in his concern caused another spike in his blood pressure, and his eyes became blurry behind his glasses. They were really starting to bother him, so he removed them and, for a second, forgot his worries. His vision had never really been that poor, but now his eyes were sharper than they had ever been. He could literally see a lizard rushing up a tree branch to a safe home for the night.

As they passed Smith's Hill Drive, his hope returned slightly as this was the way to the Southside Police Station. His hope was immediately crushed, though, as a moment later, the right to Battery Close came and went without even so much as a passing glance by the driver. They followed the curve onto Cashew City Road, and his blood pressure once again rose as he knew they were running out of road.

Just as he was seeing the end of the road and the ocean beyond, the driver made a right onto a private lane, drove passed the two houses, which were depressingly devoid of any witnesses and on down the grass to a small beach hidden there. When they arrived on the beach there was a barge with a large ramp pointed towards them that the driver then used to board the large, flat-bottomed boat.

"So…," he started, "guess we're not going to the station, huh?"

"Quiet," the Samoan growled at him from his left. "Do not move from your seat, or you will be dead before you can even think about running."

With this threat, he produced a handgun from his waistband. Seemingly content that his threat would have the desired effect, he got out of the car. His darker counterpart did the same, and they both walked over to the small pilot house on the barge; only the driver remained, and he smiled an evil smile at Hyde.

The barge pulled the ramp in, but unseen by any of the passengers, Bembe quickly darted aboard and hid amongst some fuel barrels and storage crates. Thanks to the dark that had spread and the strong breeze that evening, no one was aware of this silent and deadly stowaway.

They arrived on Paget Island, a popular destination for those with a deep love for old forts as it houses Fort Cunningham, a mere 10-minute boat ride later. As the ramp fell to the damp beach, the two men returned to the car and motioned for Hyde to exit. He stepped out in front of the two imposing figures and his fear caused another surge through his heart.

Luther was starting to realise his anxieties had risen to dangerous levels and was actively trying to calm his rapidly beating heart. He was trying to reassure himself that they would not take all of this trouble to just kill him. It was not working at all as they led him up a gravelled path towards the fort. As the decrepit edifice grew in front of them, Hyde began to feel increasingly doomed by whatever mess he had fallen into.

The orange light was glowing through the gate in front of them, and as they walked through, a large number of torches burned in holders all around the courtyard of the once stronghold of the early 1600s. Along with all of the torches was a group of about thirty people, all ranging vastly in race, size, and, of course, gender. What struck Hyde the most was the size differences in some of them, some as large as his escorts while others seemed smaller than most of his students. They walked through the centre of the throng of people and walked up in front of an even smaller group that stood at the head of the assembly. As they neared, the centre person, a beautiful woman who looked Japanese, dropped the hood that had been shielding her face from view.

"Hello, Hyde. Welcome to Fort Cunningham. I am sure you have questions, and all will be answered, we owe you this much, but first allow me to ask first: are you well? You have not been mistreated in any way?" She spoke with a slight accent, which suggested that English, while spoken with clear expertise, was her second language.

"How do you know who I am?" he asked, knowing that it was a foolish question given the disguise this group had used to procure him.

"We found out the name of the victim of the animal attack through various means." She replied with calm ease as if she were trying to calm a startled animal. "Are you well, though? It is of the utmost importance that we know you were not mistreated while you were brought here.”

“I’m fine, just less than thrilled to have been dragged out to the middle of nowhere in the middle of the night by a group of strangers. If that doctor or nurse was a relation of yours, I am deeply sorry for your loss, but I did not harm them.”

“I appreciate your condolences, but no, they were not family members of anyone here. And we already know that you are not the one responsible for their deaths. We know who it was and will be dealing with him in time.” The threat of retribution hung in the wake of her words, contrasting with her words of gratitude.

“If I am not being held accountable for their deaths, then why am I here? As I said, I do not know any of you.”

“Unfortunately, you are here because of what the one responsible has done to you. Do you understand what the thing that attacked you was yet?”

The question itself made Hyde cringe inwardly, for he had no logical theories on what his attacker could have been. He decided at the moment that since he was already fucked, he would just go with what he thought he saw.

“All I saw was a shadow, but seeing as it bit me the only explanation I can come up with is it was a wolf. Of course, I know I am thoroughly insane as there are no wolves in Bermuda, but that is what I saw.” He cringed at his own nervous rambling and awaited the ridicule. It was not forthcoming…

“No, Luther, you’re not insane. That was, in fact, a wolf you saw, but not in the sense of what you’re trying to believe it was. As crazy as it may seem, that was a Werewolf." She was so matter-of-fact in her tone that the word did not hit him properly.

"Okay, so you must clearly be crazier than I, as there is no such thing as *Werewolves*," he said derisively. In the corner of his mind, he had banished the memory, too; however, he started creeping forward to reveal details he had suppressed. The shadow was wolf-shaped but not in the canine form he had grown up reading about in books; it had longer legs than a wolf, and its head had hung down, but its muzzle appeared shorter than a wolf, and its sheer size was disproportionate to what a wolf would have. While wolves are significantly larger than their domesticated cousins, this "wolf" was much larger than even that.

"By the look in your eyes," she said coolly, "I take it you're less convinced of delusional thinking and more willing to believe the unlikely fact that you have been bitten by a Werewolf."

Hyde could not bring himself to verbally acknowledge her words, so he simply looked at her and nodded slowly.

"I do apologise from the bottom of my heart for revealing this to you," she said with genuine regret colouring her words. "And... I apologise even more for what must happen as a result of this attack..."

As her words faded, the two "constables" grabbed him under the arms and dragged him to a massive, steel-barred cage that had been hidden from view behind this "council" and threw him in it before he had any time to react.

Unbeknownst to anyone, Hyde maybe even more so, at the close proximity of the two fake constables earlier in the ride here, a change happened at the genetic level to Hyde's DNA. A change that would prove to be his saving feature from what was about to befall him.

"We cannot allow you to live, Luther," she was saying to him with tears in her eyes. "Normally, when one is bitten by one of the Fallen, they die within hours as your bodies are poisoned by the venom in our bites. Had the venom done its job, we could have focused on finding and killing your attacker, but when you awoke the next morning and were showing signs of healing, well, we knew you were part of the small percentage of people who are infected by our venom. We cannot allow a wolf to rise here. And so, unfortunately, you must die."

Without another word, the cage was lifted by a strong cable and crane and set on the bed of a small, flatbed truck. Naturally, with the threat of death imminent, Hyde began screaming for help. Alas, to no avail, as no one was close enough to the island to hear his pleas, and his captors were quite deaf to his promises and threats of retribution. He was loaded onto a barge, and a handful of his executioners accompanied him.

It was not long before Hyde realised that his screaming was doing nothing, neither garnering him assistance nor sympathy, so he stopped and attempted to accept his fate. It took them just ten more minutes to get to the deepest part of St George's Channel. Hyde's heart rate had skyrocketed through all of this, but as they grabbed his cage and slid it to the edge of the barge, it hit the level needed for the legendary transformation to happen…

All at once, the blood felt like it was going to force its way through his veins, muscles, and skin as it surged. An electrical feel surrounded his body as muscles grew beyond anything his human form could have ever produced. The elongated canines were sprouting from his mouth when the cage was unceremoniously dumped over the edge and into the cool, black waters of the Atlantic. At the touch of water, despite the changes happening, he managed to take a deep breath of air. As the weight of the cage pulled him to the depths, pure white fur began pushing through his skin, causing an unscratchable itch to cover his entire body. As his joints popped and adjusted to the change, he opened his mouth and bellowed, expelling all of the air he was trying to vainly hold in. His mouth stretched into a muzzle, eyes and ears enlarged. His claws pushed painfully through the fingernail beds of each hand as the cage slammed into the sandy bottom some forty feet from the surface. The pain being so intense that he just balled up and tried to ignore everything around him.

Oddly enough, this desire to ignore the world meant he did not notice that the air was not being crushed from his lungs, as one would expect, but instead continued to inflate and deflate as he breathed. The change in his DNA allowed him a protective lens over his eyes and his lungs to become filled with water and yet function just as they had on land, feeding him oxygen and expelling carbon dioxide. A feature that had never happened before and one he was still unaware of as he processed the pain this new body caused him. The chill of the night water was bringing him back to reality, however…

His eyes slowly opened, and he began processing just where he was, assuming that his death was imminent. Death's shroud did not cover him; instead, the combination of his enhanced vision and protective lens made the seafloor light up as if it were a cloudless day. He absorbed this and his surroundings in an instant as he looked around, finally looking down at his own body.

Aside from the shredded remains of his clothes, he had grown much taller than he had been, much taller than even his killer "constables" had been. He was now a staggering seven and a half or eight feet! His body was covered with soft, thick fur, fur the colour of the purest white snow he had ever imagined. The top of his hands were covered in fur, but his palms and fingers were now black and had the roughness that he recalled the pads of his parents' dog having. Reaching up, he touched his new face and found a long muzzle (he could only describe it as such because "nose" or "mouth" seemed too inadequate). With the proximity of his hand, he noticed the inch-and-a-half claw coming out of each finger and swallowed hard. He was now shaped like the nightmares that people wrote movies and books to; he was now the horror that went bump in the night…

He did not know how he was breathing, assuming it was because of this monster form he now was, but realised that he could not stay forever in this cage, for he was certain they would bring it back up when they assumed he had finally died. He began evaluating the cage for weakness and found the bars easily bent under his newfound strength! He bent himself a hole large enough to fit through, then swam away from the mangled metal towards the island. He knew they were on the island, and swimming there might not be best, but he was unsure where else to go; he did not want to risk running into a person and doing what all the stories had told him Werewolves (for what else could he be now?) did to those that were smaller and weaker than them. He reached the shallows of the island and scanned for potential threats on the shore before rising to just his eyes and ears breaking the surface and looking once again, thankfully nothing. He looked back out to where the barge had been and could see them standing there, patiently waiting for their victim to drown.

Hyde decided it was time to go ashore and figure out his next move. As he walked onto dry land, his eyes shifted slightly, and he had an odd feeling as if a clear eyelid were moving over his eye. He was having a tough time breathing suddenly as if starved for oxygen! He began uncontrollably coughing, large bouts of water coming up and out with each cough. Just as he thought he was going to black out from lack of air, he gasped in, and fresh air inflated his lungs!

The relief was instantaneous; he gulped in the air until the fire in his lungs finally subsided. A trickling of a theory started in his mind but was quickly silenced as a harsh whisper said: "How do you live?!"

[Chapter 3] — The Escape

Hyde's eyes shot to where the voice had come from, only to find Bembe's face looking out from between the leaves of a palmetto frond. Despite what this man had done today, he was the only one to show a semblance of "kindness" (murders aside...) towards him, and he was genuinely happy to see him.

"Where..." he started to say. It came out very coarse, like his vocal cords were rubbing on sandpaper, and then he realised his appearance might scare off his would-be saviour. It dawned on him, though, that not only did Bembe *not* run away screaming, but he also *knew* who he was!

"We may have a few things to discuss..." he answered, realising the private thoughts of the Werewolf before him. "And we can hash it all out as soon as we get out of here!"

Instead, Hyde rushed forward and pinned him to the palm tree behind him by the throat. "Try explaining why I am like this first."

His eyes darted back to the water in a panic, but he could not ignore the threat right in front of him, "I bit you because we wolves need you. You are our true leader, and I knew you were the right one! Now, I promise I will answer everything you want as soon as we are away from them!" He motioned with his head towards the water.

Hyde looked out of the corner of his eye towards his would-be killers and reluctantly released this man who had changed his life forever. Bembe kept his feet despite the long drop to the ground, looked cautiously at him and motioned for Hyde to follow him.

"I managed to find a jet-ski, but not in time to stop them from sending you overboard. I'm dying to find out how you're alive, but for now, we just need you to turn back into your human form so you can fit on the jet-ski." Bembe was talking in a low whisper, but Hyde heard him as well as if he were talking normally.

"Uh… and exactly how do I do that?!" he growled, unable to hide the annoyance.

"Right… when we get to the cove, I will show you what to do," he said, surprisingly patient.

They ran in silence after that. Bounding over roots and dodging low-hanging branches with an ease that would make any forest creature jealous. His abilities exhilarated Hyde. Having never been a particularly athletic person, running long distances and dodging things along the way would have not only proven difficult but likely his undoing. Be it stumbling due to his lack of grace or simply losing his air and heaving for relief, either of which would have likely brought the pursuers right on their trail.

But with these new enhancements they made short work of the distance between the north-east side of the island to the small cove on the western side. Bembe showing the beach with the jet-ski waiting for them.

He pulled up short, and Hyde slowed to stop behind him. After turning around to face him he said, "The best way to change back is to picture that which makes you calmest in the world and make that your sole focus, block out literally everything around you but that one thing."

Hyde was actually noticeably confident about this as his calming thing was the very thing before them. The current in the water caused a light lapping of water on the sand as minute waves struck the packed pink sand. A light breeze brought the scent of the sea to his nose. He closed his eyes and focused on the water, imagining the countless hours he spent just listening to it roll in.

"Wow… you're even better at it than I thought you would be," Bembe said incredulously.

Hyde opened his eyes, and he was no longer seeing the muzzle before his eyes nor was he looking down at the 6ft tall Bembe but rather looking up at him again as he was only 5 foot 9 in human form. His height may have stayed the same, but that was the only thing that had not changed. Looking down at his bare stomach, he saw a toned and muscled six-pack and pecks versus his former rather flabby gut he sported before this. His arms were never particularly "flabby" but were now well sculpted.

"We can get away now," Bembe urged and hopped on the jet-ski. Eager to be away from the people who wanted him dead, Hyde jumped on behind him, and they took off for the docks in St George's.

As the two were about halfway across St George's harbour, the group was pulling up the cage, certain that the extended time was enough to have killed the newly created supernatural being. Having a twisted, mangled, empty hunk of metal landing on the barge shortly after made them all quite concerned. Before the barge even made it back to shore, calls were sent out to be on the lookout for the former high school teacher turned monster.

They arrived at the docks with new issues. Hyde climbed the rubber bumpers used to keep boats from damaging themselves on the concrete and Bembe followed him, pushing the small craft back out into the current to avoid them finding out exactly where they made landfall. Bembe didn't utter a word as he passed Hyde and walked to the number of scooters parked near the cruise ship terminal (likely left by tourists), found one with the keys still in it and turned it on.

"We must hurry to the airport, Milord. Otherwise, they will surely find us in short order."

Attempting to ignore the second use of the royal moniker, Hyde jumped on the back, and they sped away, a shout from a cruise ship worker heralding their theft. But they continued without looking back.

When they hit York Street, the subterfuge with the jet-ski was shown to be for nought as three black sedans roared down the road at them, suggesting the killers were on them again. Bembe twisted the accelerator and, despite having less power than the cars, shot off away from the vehicles as they had to slow significantly on the narrow streets and tight corners. Seeing the rapid cars in the mirror, Bembe took a brief detour down Pennos Drive, took a sharp turn into parking areas, and wove the bike around buildings and fences, leaving the cars stuck behind them and needing to turn around. After passing through Penno's Wharf, they shot out onto Mullet Bay Road and sped towards the airport, the cars only a minute behind them. They could hear the screeching of tyres behind them as they desperately tried to catch up with them.

They caught up as the duo was passing through Rocky Hill Park, so Bembe took a left and ran the long way around the park, one of the cars following while the other two went to head them off. As they made the curve, however, the car tried to take the turn too fast and spun out. They continued but saw that the road was almost blocked entirely by the other two cars. As they slowed, they heard the tyres behind them start burning out as the car tried to gain purchase and follow them. Bembe waited long enough for the car to gain traction again and start barrelling after them then gunned it at the fraction of an opening left by the two cars.

"Watch this!" he cried over his shoulder to Hyde, who saw the futility of what it looked like Bembe was going to attempt. The car behind them was almost upon them when Bembe slammed on the brakes and skidded the bike into a doughnut to the left, causing the car to speed passed them and right into their comrades blocking the way. The resulting collision opened the far-right side, and Bembe gunned the engine and them through the newly opened exit. As they sped by, the remaining car executed a sharp drift to the left and came after them, he didn't catch them until just as they were entering the bridge to St David's Island. He pulled alongside them on the bridge, in the oncoming traffic lane, and the Samoan leaned out of the window and tried to grab them. Bembe managed to steer away from him, but the wall caused him to have to turn back towards the assailants. They were about halfway down the bridge when a large lorry came off the roundabout at them. Bembe saw it, but the driver of the car did not. The lorry began honking its horn and flashing its bright at the pair of speeding vehicles, but it was almost too late when the driver of the car noticed the unyielding wall bearing down on them and swerved the car to the right. It was the wrong way as they were already in the right lane, and he steered his car into the wall, busting through it and into the waters of Ferry Reach below.

With no one pursuing them anymore, Bembe drives the scooter to the Northern side of the airport where they house private planes, drives right through an open gate and up to a gulf stream sitting alone on the tarmac, engines idling causing a steady roar of noise.

"Get onboard, Sire. We need to take off immediately, or they will catch us within minutes."

Hyde was thinking of asking stupid questions like: "What about immigration?" and "Can I get dressed now," but screeching tyres sounded about a mile away, and he just ran for the ladder, Bembe a hair's breadth behind him. He turned and pulled the stairs up, and yelled for take-off. They were buckling in when the plane began taxiing onto the runway.

"How were they ready for us when we got here?" Hyde couldn't help asking.

"They have tapped into the communications of the Manō hae all over the island. When they heard we were back on the main part of the island, they likely got spun up then. They knew we were probably going to be needing to leave in a hurry."

"The mano-what?!"

"Manō hae. It's Hawaiian for "fierce shark." They control the seas and coastlines, and they do **not** like us encroaching on their territories."

They sat in silence until the plane finally reached the cruising altitude of 41,000 feet. When the aeroplane settled into a smooth flight, Bembe pointed to a small cabin at the rear of the craft.

"You'll find clothes that will fit you in there. I suggest you dress, freshen up in the lavatory, and then we can eat and discuss everything you want to know."

"You better have answers, as I am in no mood for any more games."

"I can't promise I will have every answer to every question you have, but I will be completely honest with you and any questions I do not have answers for, I will help you find them."

"Very well…"

[Chapter 4] — The Legend

Luther looked at his reflection in the mirror of the rather luxurious lavatory of the gulf stream. He marvelled at the changes he could now see in vivid detail. His now muscular body was better toned than any professional bodybuilder he had ever seen. Additionally, he was bulked up quite a bit more than before. Eat your heart out, Schwarzenegger!

He slowly wiped the sweat and grime that the night's activities had covered him in, as well as the saltwater that nearly became his grave. He pondered that part, especially as he cleaned himself off. Did becoming a Werewolf mean he was truly immortal now? No… that woman was certain that putting him underwater would mean his end, so that seemed unlikely. So, how did he survive that? As he put on the provided clothes, surprisingly well-fitting dress slacks, ruby red turtleneck, and blazer, he resolved to drag every answer out of Bembe as he could. Once dressed, he looked himself over in the mirror to ensure he looked presentable and stepped out of the cabin.

Bembe sat at a single swivel-style seat on the starboard side, working on a laptop. Hyde made it a point to walk up quietly, looking over his shoulder at the screen and catching a glimpse of a secure messaging service before taking a seat on the couch on the port side of the aeroplane and facing Bembe.

All pretence was out of his voice as he said, "Now we're alone and safe. Talk. And it better be good…" He let the tone of the threat hang in the air to impress upon Bembe that doing anything less might mean his life.

Catching the tone and subsequent threat, Bembe hit sent on his email and slowly closed his laptop. His heart was heavy with fear as he turned to the agitated creature to his left.

"I will answer everything I can; I swear it upon my life, Milord."

"Well, let's start with that: why have you been calling me 'Milord' and 'Sire'?"

"Because according to our traditions, you are now the lord, the king if you will, of all Werewolves, the Argentum Lupus." He said this with a sense of reverence.

Recognising the Latin from his teaching, he said, "Silver Wolf?"

"An epitaph we earned in the early days. Most of us hunt at night for obvious reasons; well, those who saw us in moonlight began calling us that. Sadly, it also fed the legend of silver being lethal to us. It is no more lethal than any other metal to the Argentum."

"I see… okay, so why me? Why was I attacked and bitten?"

"The legend of the Alpha has long spoken of the characteristics present in an Alpha. Certain things are present in an Alpha and in no other living creature. The most notable is the specific stripe of silver that runs through the hair of an Alpha. They are born with it."

"But mine didn't show up until my hair began to darken in my mid-twenties." Hyde protested.

"Your silver was there but was hidden due to the stark white hair you grew up with. The other sign was your eyes, they are a unique shade of blue with silver specks in them. Lastly, you were born during a blue moon. All of these signs led me to you. I am terribly sorry for the bite, but it was truly the only way, as you were not born an Argentum."

"Is that typically how Werewolves happen?"

"That is the only way they are allowed! Biting humans for the sake of turning them has been outlawed, as less than one percent live through the process."

"So, you sought me out, stalked me, bit me illegally, all in the hopes that I am this, Alpha? That seems a ridiculous thing to lay your hope in."

"Right now, the Argentum have been fighting against one another for centuries. The "leadership," if that's what you want to call it, has only been focusing on itself. They do not care that we are fractured into small sub-Packs, nor do they care about the Werefolk that make up the realm's subjects. The Alpha unites the Pack, and we have not had an Alpha since the last one was poisoned in 1623."

"Poisoned? How?"

"It was always said to us that the Ursa poisoned him to gain an advantage in the North, but I do not believe this. I think he was assassinated by one of the Elders so that they could regain control over the Pack."

"The Ursa?"

"I apologise. I keep forgetting that you are ignorant of our world. Allow me to start at the beginning.

"In the winter of 752 B.C., during a total solar eclipse, Comet West passed by Earth. Something happened in the shadow of the eclipse. The shadow passed over northern Gaul, what is now modern Germany. During that time, eight women gave birth to eight vastly different children. They all seemed like normal, healthy babies, but they were far from the 'normal' their parents were hoping for. When each child reached the age of 6, whenever they would lose control of their emotions and the adrenalin spiked, like what you experienced tonight, they would turn into their animal side. Each child represents the most common predators in Germany: badger, fox, otter, wildcat, lynx, bear, shark, and wolf. The three largest became the ruling class over the remaining five. It is believed that while these first eight were the very first of our species, they more or less opened the way for others to become Werefolk. There were new members, first before the founding members were old enough to begin breeding, then others were being born that were far from the beginning. As numbers began to swell, we formed what we call the Underkingdoms. We became the Argentum Lupus, the bears became the Ursa, and the sharks did not have a name but later were called the 'Manō hae.' The Manō hae had no desire for anything on land and, seeing as no one could oppose them there, receded to their coastlines and deep places. Naturally territorial, the Argentum and Ursa began feuding immediately for control. None of us can match the Ursa for strength, but we have much superior numbers, so neither side has a significant advantage over the other.

"But with our Pack as fractured as it has been, we have been losing ground to the Ursa. It will not be long before we lose Grimlecht, the Werewolf capital city in Germany. Those that control the Capital control the Werefolk."

There was a pregnant silence that hung between the two men as Hyde attempted to process this new information. It seemed so incredible to border the insane, but seeing as he did transform into a massive, anthropomorphic wolf once already, he figured he could not be throwing around a word like "insane" in this situation.

"Why is it I have never heard of the Ursa or the Manō hae? At least in one form or another, like Argentum?"

"The Ursa's lower numbers and more even temperaments have allowed them to avoid being seen a lot, therefore preventing themselves from being cast in many horror stories like we are. And technically, you have heard of the Manō hae; you just would have more associated them with the lost city of Atlantis and mermaids."

"Ah, that makes a lot of sense, actually. That makes far more sense than the theory of mermaids being developed from manatees!" Hyde could not help but chuckle at his little revelation. The laughter helped ease some of the tension that had been shot into his muscles by the day's chaos.

"Wait a minute, I have been going for over 24 hours now. Running, dodging, attempted drowning… why am I not exhausted?" Hyde asked, perplexed.

"While we can be killed, and frankly, you should be dead, we are immortal. You will never age, and your need for sleep disappeared when you underwent your first change."

"So, what they were trying to do… drown me," the words stuck in Hyde's throat a bit, "should have killed me? I just assumed that now that I am a monster, I was immune to things like that."

"Firstly, we're *not* monsters. Do we look terrifying? Absolutely. But we do not prey on humans. If we're doing what we're supposed to, they should never know what we are. But to answer your question, yes, you should be a corpse by now. I have no explanation as to how you survived.

"Werefolk is notoriously difficult to kill, this is true, but shoot enough bullets into vital parts of any of us, and we *will* die. Werefolk heal very rapidly, shoot one in the arm and it will likely be closed and healed within 10 minutes. But severe trauma? Pine box time. And yes, drowning is definitely on the list."

"So, barring someone slipping me a nasty Mickey or wiping the floor with me using a cannon, I will live… forever?" Immortality was a philosophical question he had discussed with friends at length. He had always felt mixed emotions about it; on the one hand, he had a longing to see where the world would be in the future, but on the other hand, he did not relish living beyond the friends and family he had.

Seemingly reading his thoughts, Bembe solemnly said, "Your friends and family will need to believe you dead. If not for your protection, their own."

Hyde opened his mouth to protest, but the logic slammed into him almost immediately. This life does not allow for fragile connections. Hell, if the truth about his new… condition?... they may very well try to end him out of fear or sheer envy. And that was not even considering the complications of potential enemies using them against him. Thankfully, Hyde had always lived a bachelor's existence, eliminating any potential partners or children needing to be taken care of. He had lost both parents to the Covid-19 pandemic, and he was an only child. Really the only family he had left was an aunt and her husband, and a few cousins. He had always been very fond of them but was not seriously close to any of them. The loss was more keenly felt at the loss of his friends, who all had become surrogate family members.

Hyde resolved that for this to happen to anyone, he was likely the best candidate. His loss would be felt but not by very many, and he felt they would all manage well in his absence.

"So, tell me about this, Grimlecht. Is that where we are going?"

"The Argentum will celebrate the return of an Alpha, but no, not yet. First, we need to go and talk to my Pack leader in Cuba. She controls the Central American Pack and is the real reason why I came to find and turn you. She had me research records all over the world to find the Alpha. She had no idea if you existed yet, but the situation with the Argentum and the Ursa has gotten so bad, she was grasping for anything."

"Being an island, won't the Manō hae find us there?"

"Our Pack leader actually was the first Werefolk to be born in Cuba, so the Manō hae see it as her territory and leave it alone. Truthfully, the Manō hae is the most peaceful of the Werefolk. But I trespassed into one of their territories and, on top of that offence, bit and turned one of the humans under their protection. It was a truly awful offence to them."

"Can we appease them somehow?"

"Appeasement is not really our way…"

"You said the way things have gone is not working, sounds like we may need to try a new way. The definition of insanity is 'repeating an action and expecting a different result', after all."

Bembe looked Hyde in the eye with a sense of loyalty that caught Hyde off guard. Bembe said nothing, but the look clearly conveyed that whatever misgivings Bembe may have had towards this mythical "leader" evaporated at that moment.

[Chapter 5] — The Cuban Elder

Hyde wanted time to process everything he had heard, so he asked for time to eat. Bembe said the galley was stocked with sandwiches and drinks and asked what he could get him. The concept of being served did not sit well with him, however, so he said he would go looking for his own dinner.

After finding a sandwich and drink, Hyde sat away from Bembe to consider the life he now has. He had never been one to aspire for more than what his station was in life. As a child, he was well-liked by his classmates but never considered himself one of the "popular" kids. This carried on into high school where he did well in class and some sports for the track and field competitions but was never what one would consider to be a "star" athlete or pupil. He did graduate in the top five percent at Cambridge when he sought his degree in education.

His focus was always more on developing strong relationships with peers, and many if not most, would say he was a savagely loyal friend. Thinking of this renewed the sting of loss he felt about losing his friends. Additionally, it was extremely important to him that he be a well-liked teacher. Not to the point of being a push-over, but one that the students enjoyed learning from.

Due to these being his focus, he was well-liked and respected as a teacher and friend, and this was perfect for him. He did not desire to be a world renowned professor or be a ground-breaking leader in education, just teach his students. Now he was being expected to be a "ruler" … he had difficulty grasping this.

Static from the overhead interrupted his inner musings, "We're descending to José Martí International Airport at this time, so we ask that you please remain seated and buckled until we come to a complete stop. It is a balmy 86 degrees and clear skies. Thank you."

Hyde tried to prepare himself for meeting an Elder. Bembe told him she had lived over 500 years, born only a year after Columbus conquered the island and stole it from the indigenous. Hyde felt nothing could properly prepare him for this meeting.

As the plane filled with supernatural beings landed and the occupants prepared to board a smaller plane bound for Isla de la Juventud, a young woman opened her eyes and looked out from her balcony and across the Gulf of Batabano towards where the two companions were. Despite knowing the fight yet to come, she breathed a sigh of relief, for she knew her son had been successful in his mission. The Alpha had arrived, and he would help settle their tumultuous world.

The twin-prop AT72 landed on the runway of Rafael Cabrera Airport at 10:52 a.m. with no issues. The two men deplaned and were promptly escorted away from the other passengers to a blue 1951 Buick convertible waiting for them. A brief drive north, they came across a large, gated road leading into the forest near Playa Colombo. The driver pulled up to the ancient-looking speaker box mounted in front of the gate and reached out to press the button. Despite its age, an extremely clear voice speaking Spanish asked them who they were and to state their business. Hyde's Spanish was horrendous, but he did catch his name and "Alpha" being said in return by the driver. The voice responded in an almost reverent tone and said in heavily accented English:

"Greetings, Lord Luther. Our leader, Lisandra Castillo de Romero, welcomes you graciously to our home."

As the voice fades, the gate slowly swings in, revealing a long, overgrown dirt road. The trees grew over the road, turning the drive into a dark green tunnel. As the road snakes back to the left, they are welcomed by a field of neatly trimmed grass with raised flower beds lining the now cobblestone drive. Palm trees are placed between the flower beds and there is a hill about halfway down the road that is hiding whatever "home" the voice was speaking of. At the crest of the hill, they looked down upon a sprawling and luxurious villa. Easily a size to rival the White House, the terracotta-roofed mansion stood with a commanding view of the ocean behind it, a large horse stable with white fenced-in corrals to the left, an Olympic-sized swimming pool to the right, and a large circular driveway in front that was currently holding what appeared to be hundreds of people in fine clothing.

"I am underdressed, it seems…" he mumbled.

"Your finery is not in your clothes but your character, Sire. Be yourself, and you will stand above those you see here."

This was clearly meant to be a comforting statement, but it disquieted him a great deal. Luther was not a monarch. He had lived under the quiet rule of Queen Elizabeth II for his entire life, and while she was no dictator, he had always loathed the idea of a monarchy. The path to greed, power-hungry, and fear of losing that power was all too easy of a road to take. And what's more, once one goes down that path… it was highly unlikely that they would turn from it.

He followed the tall Cuban out of the car, and as Bembe stepped to the right, Hyde spotted a short woman with reddish, bronze skin and long, flowing hair the colour of the darkest night blowing lightly in the tropical breeze. His gaze involuntarily started to size her up, she was very fit and had a commanding presence in her stance, full lips with no lipstick and high, unadorned cheeks. When he saw her eyes, he was shocked to find them the richest hue of gold he had ever seen. Once his eyes met hers, he could not look anywhere else. Though she was an unmatched beauty, her appearance was lost on him, as her eyes spoke of centuries of knowledge and experience. This was a woman who tolerated little and expected much from anyone she met.

Her voice flowed like a honeyed wine, rich in an accent that Hyde had never heard before, "My Lord, I humbly greet you and welcome you to the home of the Central American Pack. I had heard of your troubles with the Manō hae, but it pleases me greatly to see you are unharmed by the sea dwellers. Despite all you have been through, however, we have much yet to discuss."

"Thank you for having me. I do not wish to offend you; what may I call you?" Hyde spoke with deference to this leader as she seemed to emanate an air demanding respect.

Her golden eyes brightened at the show of respect, though her face remained a mask; he was respectful, but she knew all too well the ploys of men wishing to make her subservient to them. Nevertheless, his deference to her could not go unnoticed.

"Thank you, Milord. You may call me Lisandra or Sancra for short if you please." She spoke this with a slight, guarded smile. She wanted to show this newcomer that he was safe but did not dare bare her neck to the one who may yet step on it.

Not wishing to be the one to stand on ceremony, especially one he did not believe in, Hyde said, "Then please forgo this 'Lord' business then. I understand there is a hierarchy here, but I do not wish to be held to such a level, much less one I have yet to have earned."

Again, pleasing words to her ears. She recalled the arrogance of his predecessor well, though, so she did not allow sugared words to easily sway her into trusting him.

"As you wish, sir. For now, please rest and wash the travels away. We will have dinner tonight and discuss the future we are hoping for us all."

As Hyde and Bembe walked to the rooms she had prepared for them, her mind wandered to the last time an Alpha graced her home.

An April moon hung low in the sky as he stepped from the carriage. He stood an immense six foot ten inches tall, an unheard-of size for any human, and she knew it was the height of his father. The silver streak in his hair reflected the moonlight and gave him a majestic mystique about him.

"Lisandra." His thick English accent is butchering her name, though she was surprised he even bothered to learn her name given her heritage and skin tone. Women were not highly regarded in 1622 after all, regardless of if they were human or Werefolk.

The surprise was quickly mollified by decorum, and she simply said, "Greetings, Milord."

Her shock had not gone unnoticed, though he refused to acknowledge her more than was absolutely necessary. Having been born to a landowner whose family would later become the Baron Camoys gave the man both nobility and intolerance for any below his station. This "leader" was certainly beneath him as she was a woman and only commanded a few dozen Argentum in this… "New World". The world may have shifted in size since his birth, but these savages would not change social conventions so long as he had anything to do with it.

"Where is my ship and its cargo?"

"As I said in the dispatch, Milord, the ship had been spotted near Nassau about a month and a half ago, but nothing has been said of it since. I am afraid the likelihood of pirates having taken it is far too high to believe anything else."

"I told you it was to be found, not excuses for it being lost to be bandied about."

"I have scouts all over the Caribbean looking for her Sire. Should they spot her, we will know within a couple of days."

"You expect me to sleep in this squalor for *days*?!"

Stealing a quick glance around the rapidly growing home, she inwardly acknowledged it was not likely to equate the usual niceties he was so accustomed to, but it was far from squalor.

"It is the best home you will find in all of Cuba, Milord. I do offer my humblest apologies that it is not as luxurious as you deserve, but I believe it will serve you well for the short time you are here."

"I will not be staying here," he said dismissively, "I would sooner return to my ship. Send word the moment you have heard. I do not wish to spend one more day here longer than absolutely necessary."

Without another word, he pivoted on his heel and boarded the carriage he had departed only moments before. He had barely sat before the crack of the whip and squeal of frightened horses rushed the posh carriage off her estate as quickly as they had arrived.

She knew fully of his contempt for her. She had been told by many passing Rogues, Argentum that insisted on living alone, of this generation's Alpha. Born into a wealthy landowner's home the summer of 902 A.D., he had had the silver spoon promptly shoved down his throat since they named him, of which was lost to time as he would only go by the sobriquet of "Baron". His reputation of outspoken distaste for anyone not of noble birth was widely known. His massive size and matching strength, mixed with the fact that he was the Alpha, were the only facts staving off his assassination.

His incessant need to become embroiled in the most heinous of industries also made him very despised by his subjects. This most recent foray into slavery was one she found particularly abhorrent. While the deep-seated need to be loyal to her Lord was fighting her desire to do the right thing constantly, she tipped the scales in her favour by gaining the unlikely assistance of a young Manō hae that went by the name of Black Caesar, the infamous lieutenant of the famed pirate captain: Edward Teach, also known as, Captain Blackbeard. The pirates agreed to take possession of the Baron's "cargo" for a nominal fee, which she was happy to pay. The problem at the moment, however, was they were supposed to scuttle the ship so it would not be found by anyone, especially the Baron, but before they could, a small group of pirates off Blackbeard's own ship sailed away from them, and they were currently chasing them north towards the American colonies.

It was actually five days before word came that the *Queen Anne's Revenge* had caught up to them just south of La Florida and sunk them. During that time, true to his word, the Baron never left his vessel, choosing instead to send his own servants and slaves to gather anything he required. Ultimately, she had to board the longboat to his ship.

Once aboard, she found the Baron on the quarterdeck with a large, embellished table laden with enough food to feed some of the small villages here. He was taking a small bite out of a local *Tostones* that smelled delicious to her as she walked up to his table. He spit it onto the deck and hurled the entire plate over the side.

"I am *sick* of this fucking country!" he raged. "You had better be here with pleasing tidings, or you may find yourself tied to my anchor…" He left the threat hanging there.

Undaunted, she replied, "No, Milord. We just received news that a ship matching the markings of your ship was set upon by a ship sailing under the black flag of pirates."

He did not move nor speak. His visage became stone for a hairsbreadth of a moment before he transformed into the immense eight-foot wolf in the blink of an eye. Even with her own formidable speed and strength, he caught her completely off-guard, and before she could register that he had moved, he had her by the throat, dangling her feet over the turquoise waters below. His white pelt with jet-black stripes running the length of his back rippled in anticipation of her reacting to this aggression. Argentum was not permitted to attack one another, and even the Alpha was held to that law, so she refrained from changing, knowing that he would use that fact as justification for her death.

"You really are as useless as the badgers. I do not wish to hear any more excuses from your lips. Pray I never return to this godforsaken spit of land again, for if I do, I will kill you."

Without warning, he dropped her into the sea. As she swam to the surface, the ship had already exploded with activity as sailors scurried to put the vessel to sea. An island native, she was not upset by the impromptu swim back to her home; she simply swam leisurely back to the beach.

She had never seen him again after this encounter, as he was killed the following year in Massachusetts. While many within the Argentum suspected the Ursa of poisoning him, she tended to lean more with the more common belief that the English Puritans eliminated the snobbish reminder of the land they fled from. At least she truly hoped the ironic death was true.

The ancient grandfather clock chimed six times to let the world know it was 6 o'clock and time for dinner. She made her way to the dining hall, stopping before the closed doors and motioning for the attendants to hold. She wanted to suppress any preconceived notions she may have towards this Alpha. He deserved to be judged on his own character and not by the actions of a fool centuries prior to his birth. With a strong nod of her head, she cleared the memory from her mind and alerted the attendants she was ready to enter.

[Chapter 6] — Finding An Ally

The doors at the front of the room opened, and in swept this petite, yet fierce woman. She paused in front of Hyde long enough to do a small curtsy and welcome him again to her home, then walked to the head of the table; she hesitated and glanced at him briefly, considering allowing him the place of honour. Her glance was met with a slight shaking of his head, signalling that he did not wish to place himself in her obvious place. She took it as confirmation to her own thoughts of what he had said earlier about not earning such accolades yet. She silently appreciated his humble nature.

They sat in silence while food was brought out to them. She knew he had not come from wealth, so she had requested the chef prepare more modest fare than was regularly served to visiting dignitaries. While modest, a fantastic meal was laid out before them, and they ate in silence, content to get past the meal before diving into what was promising to be an extremely heavy discussion. As the remaining dishes are cleared, everyone steels themselves for whatever this meeting may bring about.

"So, I am certain you have many questions," she said, starting the conversation.

"I do," he replied earnestly. "Bembe has filled me in on somewhat of the history and slightly glossed over the 'why me' part. What can a high school teacher from an island significantly smaller than this one, much less the sheer size of the world I have been informed of, do for any of this?"

"Your humble beginnings will actually serve you well in this new position you have been thrust into. I understand that this is all so very overwhelming for you, but as a teacher, I am sure you know and grasp that famous Shakespearean saying: 'Some are born great, some achieve greatness, and others have greatness thrust upon them.' You were born to a lovely yet modest set of parents. Your father was a constable, and you followed your mother's footsteps into teaching. These professions are inherently selfless careers, and I am certain they instilled some wonderful values in you."

"You are assuming a great deal..." Hyde did not wish to disparage his parents to strangers, but he could not ignore the fact that his father was a great constable and served the people of Bermuda with distinction, but also was a raging alcoholic who was sometimes very verbally abusive to him and his mother. His mother was a wonderful mother and teacher, but she was as meek and mild of a person as ever you'd meet. All in all, they gave him a sense of duty and integrity, self-esteem issues, and depression.

"This is fair, and I have read of your father's misdeeds from your therapist's notes," she said flatly while eyeing him, testing to see if he had an explosive temper that was far too common with "leaders" within the Argentum. His light blue eyes boiled with anger, but it did not boil over.

Through gritted teeth, he said, "Invading my privacy is not the best tact in getting one's help with anything."

Inwardly, she was smiling despite the fact that she had just poked a severely dangerous opponent. He was reserved and respectful but not incapable of anger and standing up for what he believed was right. These were characteristics of herself that she valued highly.

To attempt to mollify his anger, she said, "I do apologise for that, for truly it was never my intent to violate your privacy in such a manner. But I am risking lives simply talking to you, so I needed to be sure you were worth the potential deaths."

The attempt was not only successful in assuaging his anger, but it also humbled him. Hyde knew that whenever strong, opposing politics clashed, there was tension, but he had not considered the devastation that his rise to power might cause.

His concern moved him immediately into caution for those around him, "Are you certain this is the best move then? Am I worth the lives of countless others to you?"

"Loss of any lives will be tragic, but there are lives being lost constantly with the Pack being splintered the way it has been. With an Alpha getting the Pack back under control and uniting us all, not only would we stop fighting each other, but also be able to defend against the Ursa, who work tirelessly to supplant us in our territories." She tried in vain to withhold the desperation in her voice but was unable to stop it from tinting her words.

"Why is there so much infighting? And how can I stop it?"

"The other Elders have all grown greedy or disinterested in maintaining the younger wolves coming in. Lacking proper guidance and true leadership, and the new wolves become arrogant with how strong they are. This causes them to test each other and some of the older wolves. This causes the older wolves to either lash out violently at the youngers to the point of becoming killers of their own kind, or they give the younger wolves a 'pack' with which to 'belong' to further divide us."

"That doesn't exactly explain how me, one man, is going to be able to quell literal *centuries* of bloodshed." He felt a sense of duty, but this task was beyond his knowledge.

"The presence of an Alpha is, in of itself, unifying for most. Your position affords you physical strength that is more than any wolf, Elder or not. Werefolk respect strength."

"People fear physical strength, not respect it. And if physical strength were enough, the previous Alpha would still be here, right or wrong?"

She hated it, but she said, "Right. But I believe you possess something that no other Alpha has before you."

"Sarcastic wit?" he said dryly.

Despite herself, she chuckled at the jape, "No, you possess compassion and true leadership potential. It is obvious when one looks at your teaching history: no disciplinary actions against you, a 100% passing rate with 80% averaging over a B+, letters of commendation, and awards for commitment to your students. You may believe you are average, but your actions make you amazing."

Everything she said was true, though Hyde never focused on his accomplishments. He always felt that the awards were a waste of time, for he did not do what he did for accolades or praise. He became the teacher he had always wanted to have when he was in school. Someone who didn't just stand in front of the class and lecture on the various subjects but rather someone who wanted those he taught to understand these things and, more importantly, why it was so vital we learned them.

"I will grant you that I am a great teacher, but I still have doubts about how well that is going to help stop killers and despots," he relented.

"I have lived in this world my entire life, and that is no small amount of time; I will teach you the politics and customs. Bembe will teach you how to be the wolf you are."

Hyde looked over at Bembe, who was grinning from ear to ear. "I have a full lesson planned out for you, sir. It helps that you are such a natural at transforming," at this, he turned to Lisandra, "He was able to return to human form within seconds. Literally, the fastest I have ever heard of."

Lisandra was visibly impressed, though cautioned, "Instinct in the heat of the moment will always come easier than when you are calm and have time to think about what you are doing."

Hyde nodded in agreement. He had no idea about any of this, but he knew that a creature's fight or flight response gave one an edge when in a dangerous situation.

"This is going to take a long time…" Hyde observed.

"Fortunately, we do not sleep. We can lie down and do what amounts to deep meditation, but we cannot fully sleep anymore. As we have supernatural strength and endurance, we can train you day and night at a very accelerated rate."

Hyde was no stranger to hard work, but this sounded like torture…

[Chapter 7] — Sparring With an Alpha

"**S**on of a fucking bitch!" Hyde roared as Bembe once again got under his guard and opened the skin of his stomach just enough to bleed him but not wound him too grievously.

It had been weeks since the dinner with Lisandra, and while he had improved, the far superior Bembe had been trouncing him far more often than he liked. The lessons had been gruelling right out of the gate, with a sparring match to test his combat abilities. He had a fair amount of hand-to-hand experience from being a young boy and man that refused to take too much shit from others. But lacking someone trying to kill him, he had never been truly tested before. As such, his victories over bullies and smart-mouthed wise-asses meant that he was not prepared for what he faced and was defeated relatively quickly.

Bembe had told him that he would not strike deeply but would cause him injury to help train the younger man through his pain. Hyde was instructed not to hold back in any way whatsoever, however. They healed rapidly but a strike that would normally be considered "lethal" risked delaying his training as it took hours to heal to full strength. Hyde felt his instruction was a bit condescending until he stepped into the sand ring behind the stable and tried to kill this man before him. Try as he may, Hyde could not strike nor catch the graceful killer.

They remained in human form the first few weeks, as Bembe wanted Hyde used to not relying on his stronger wolf form. At the start of the sixth week, though, Bembe had him turn before they sparred. It was more difficult to become the wolf than it was to turn back to human, Hyde found. Unleashing his inner wolf meant that Hyde had to tap into his survival response and cause his heart to race.

"Imagine what it felt when those Manō hae were loading you into the cage and dropping you over the edge of the boat," Bembe instructed.

"I had never felt surer in my life that I was about to die. That is not exactly the sort of experience I'd like to relive…"

"Do not worry; once you get used to turning, you won't have to relive the feeling. It will become almost like flexing a muscle. As easily as you turned last time, I have a feeling that analogy will prove most accurate. The change happens when we consciously tap into our adrenalin rather than relying on instinct to do it for us."

"So, adrenalin is the key?"

"More like a trigger," he explained. "The adrenalin flows through our central nervous… honestly, I do not fully understand the science behind it; I just know that a heaping amount of adrenalin is needed to trigger the change."

Hyde considered this information as he forced himself to think back to that experience over a month in the past. He remembered feeling afraid, terrified even, and he could feel his pulse quicken. The beating of his heart was not fast enough to trigger the change,

but he noticed something he had never felt before. He felt this…
place within himself. It was clearly new to him, but it also felt almost
familiar. He focused on it and felt a bigger surge than he did a second
ago, which exhilarated him. He "pushed" against it even more and
the surge was explosive, so much in fact that he changed
immediately. Within an instant, he went from stocky man to graceful
wolf, his clothes falling to shredded ruins around him. So rapid was
his change that even Bembe jumped back in alarm, triggering his
own change.

Standing to his new full height of 8 feet, he flexed his muscles
and marvelled at the tightened strands of this new form. He had not
gotten the opportunity to explore this new body the last time he had
turned due to the need to run for their lives, but he was enjoying the
change now! Having always been an out-of-shape nerd, Hyde had
never been very athletic. When it was track and field day, he had
done decently at the field sports and absolutely despised the track
sports. Hyde actually placed well in throwing the shot put and
discus, but when it came to running… well, let it suffice that he did
not enjoy that aspect of life in athletics.

That was all in his past now, though, as he crouched low,
bunching his leg muscles until releasing the energy stored and
leaping a solid 30 feet straight up and landing with almost no sound
and even less effort. He grinned inwardly before bounding forward
in a run that made him blur from the sheer speed, ripping the ground
up from the force he drove into it. Bembe's brown and black form
appeared next to him within a second, which spurred a spontaneous
bout of competitiveness within him, and he pushed to go even faster.
Even with his own formidable speed, as he was one of the fastest
amongst the Werefolk, Bembe was put in the dust so quickly it made
him stare in awe at the white blur that shot ahead.

Werefolk are naturally much stronger and faster than humans, given their amalgamation with the animal kingdom. The typical speed of a Werewolf is going to be faster than a Werebadger, but they all move quite a bit faster than human beings. The fastest man has ever achieved has been 27.78 miles per hour, set by world record holder Usain Bolt. A true glory to mankind, but a normal wolf can hit speeds of up to 37 miles per hour, which pales that accomplishment when put together. A Werewolf, being part man and part wolf, combines these numbers and hits an average of about 52 miles per hour, with Bembe outpacing that even further by hitting speeds of 60 miles per hour. Hyde ran even faster than this, hitting speeds in excess of 75 miles per hour.

Hyde darted around the grounds of the villa with wild abandon, completely enthralled by his newly acquired speed and unbelievable stamina, as he was not short of breath in the slightest. His enhanced reflexes also gave him astonishing agility as every would-be obstacle was spotted, assessed, and avoided without even thinking about it. Seeing his trainer back at the start he turned back, leaping over the entire stables in the process. Finally, sprinted back to the training yard and slid to a stop in front of the awed Bembe.

"Well! I guess you can handle the change quite fantastically, and it seems!" he was chuckling while he spoke, still in wonder over the impromptu display of speed.

"I could feel this… place within me, and when I focused on it, the surge was electrifying!"

"To my knowledge, no one, not even the Alphas that came before you, could reach the change that easily or that rapidly! It usually takes about thirty seconds roughly for most to fully change, but you did it almost instantly! I can't believe how you did that!"

"Would it be strange to say that it felt natural to me? Like it was something I have been meant to do all of my life?"

"I do not believe it to be strange, but it is unexpected. However, I have never spoken to an Alpha about it either. Alphas are always stronger than the rest of us, and it stands to reason that you would have abilities that exceed our own."

"What are the strengths of the Argentum?"

"We have increased strength, speed, and reflexes. Our senses of smell, sight, and hearing are significantly higher than almost every other Werefolk. Werebadgers have a much better sense of smell than us. Werefoxes can see better than we can, and the Werelynxes have the best hearing out of us all."

"You had mentioned that there were others but never specified them before. Why are they not Underkingdoms of their own?"

"I will actually let Senora Romero explain all of that to you. She was hoping you would take a break from training with me to train on the politics soon anyway. But how about a little bit of sparring session in wolf form?"

Boosted by the thought of his new form's abilities, Hyde responded by simply dropping into a combat stance and emitting a deep, rumbling growl that actually made Bembe hesitate. Sensing the fear, Hyde leapt at the older warrior. Hyde intended to use his moment of surprise to finally score a hit on the more experienced hunter, but despite his initial hesitation, Bembe was still too skilled to be completely taken unaware. At the last possible second, Bembe dodged away from the outstretched claw, luckily so as Hyde misjudged the distance and would have caused serious harm and twisted to put his jaws on the back of Hyde's neck, but before he could pin the younger wolf into quick submission, Hyde snapped his head forward out of the jaws, used his other hand to turn his body back on itself allowing him to kick Bembe across the field. While not the "lethal" hit Bembe was trying to teach him, it was a solid hit that effectively put Bembe at the mercy of the Alpha, and Hyde capitalised on it by rushing forward and pinning Bembe to the ground with a massive, clawed hand around his throat.

"I yield, Milord," Bembe said with reverence, appreciative of the young Alpha's natural combat skill. "You still have a long road ahead of you, but you have good natural skill, especially in wolf form. Try not to rely on it too much; however, while you do change quickly, a fight can be over in the blink of an eye, and that is too fast even for you."

They took their break at that and went their separate ways, Bembe voicing a reminder of how to turn back to human form. Hyde nodded in acknowledgement and trotted away to his room. After a brief introspective, he turned back to human form and went to bathe the dirt from his skin before donning the fresh clothes left in his room.

[Chapter 8] — The Underkingdoms

After grabbing a bite to eat in the kitchen that seemed to be going 24/7, he went and knocked on the door to Lisandra's study. She opened the door and welcomed him into the expansive room; his eyes roamed the room. The walls were over 20 feet high and lined with bookshelves that were floor to ceiling and stuffed with modern and ancient texts alike. In the centre of the room, a large oak desk with a leather executive chair. Two dark brown leather wingback chairs sat in front of the fireplace, currently holding a small fire that was the sole light source. She gestured for him to sit in one of the wingback chairs, and she took her place across from him.

"I know you have been told the basic history of our very existence and that history will serve enough for that aspect of our beginnings. What I must instruct you on now is the various politics that exist with the entirety of the Werefolk." She sighed before starting, alluding to the sheer unnecessary fact that politics was encroaching on them. "Humans have their own politics as you well know, but ours are different in that we must step in the right places with people that can live forever. A minor slight that is allowed to fester for centuries can easily become a full-on war at any moment.

This is why the need of a wise, benevolent Alpha is so desperately needed.

"As you already know, the three Apex predators make up the controlling factions of the Underkingdoms. Each has a strength that has permitted us to make the remaining five Werefolk subservient to us. This is an aspect I fully disagree with, just so you know my stance on it. I was born a year after Columbus came and conquered my people; I have seen first-hand the disgusting nature of bending a people to your will."

He nodded and said, "Fortunately, our minds are as one on this issue. I have never believed in the *ruling* of people through means of force or fear."

"I appreciate this fact," she said warmly, truly pleased that this Alpha was agreeing with something she felt the strongest about. "That being said, the current leaders of the Argentum do not agree with us. It is their belief that since we are stronger and outnumber all of the other groups, then we *should* be in control. Just to be clear, we are *not* the strongest, nor do we possess the greatest of numbers. Those honours go to the Ursa and the Manō hae, respectively. The only reason these two are unable to wipe us out for our sheer arrogance is because one is more solitary than we are, and the other cares for little out of its watery empire. The Ursa generally roam the planet individually, and the Manō hae stay on the seas.

"The Ursa are by far the strongest physically of all of the Werefolk. One-on-one, an Argentum would be killed by even their weakest sub-type, the Pandas. I know you have even more strength than likely our strongest and even you would struggle against one of them. Their strongest sub-type, the Polars, is said to have the strength to crack the ground beneath them, and they are known for their short tempers. Fortunately, their governing body is made up of a council featuring each sub-type but headed up by a member of the sub-type, Norther-American Black. She is extremely level-minded and fair. Her name is Sokanon, and I have dealt with her before.

"In terms of sheer numbers, the Manō hae have all other groups beat for their people live in every ocean, and some in lakes and rivers. They are very capable of banding together and could wipe us all out, but they are peace-loving despite their terrifying animal side. All they have ever wanted was to be left alone, and for the most part, they have been. Other Werefolk unfortunately cross paths with them on occasion, and the results are always the same: death for the land Werefolk. The Manō hae defend their territories and privacy with unwavering strength. Some of their sub-types actually do rival the Ursa in terms of physical strength, but where the Ursa will band together to assist one another, those Manō hae that are that strong utterly refuse to work with each other.

"The other five are the Werebadgers, Werefoxes, Wereotters, Werecats, and Werelynxes. Each group is put into a type of class system based on their strengths; the Werebadgers are at the bottom of the classes; they are industrious people and, therefore, make up the workers within the two land Underkingdoms. The Werefoxes are known for their sly nature and quick hands; they are all thieves. The Wereotters are mischievous to their very core, and being able to utilise the water effectively, they are smugglers. Werecats are the only Werefolk whose animal form is not anthropological. When they turn, they turn into slightly larger versions of just about any cat you can imagine. Thanks to that ability, they are used as spies. Lastly, the Werelynxes… the stealthiest out of every Werefolk, and therefore every creature on the planet; they use this skill as assassins. If one comes for you, pray you spot them first, or it will be your last day of life."

"Why are they not considered an Apex and have their own Underkingdom?" he asked.

"While they are very powerful, some have been known to have killed an Ursa before, and they are the fewest in number."

"That makes sense," he nodded.

"As skilled as each of them is, none of them possess the raw physical strength of the three Apex. As such, they have been beaten and pushed into serving the two land Underkingdoms in particular. To my knowledge, the Manō hae do not use any of the Support Five for anything and do treat them better than the Ursa and Argentum do, but still not as they deserve."

"I see. Well, you clearly have a lot of respect for them and obviously want them treated better. Have you tried making changes yourself?"

"I am well respected and even have good relations with all of the Werefolk, but my respect and appreciation of the Support Five has caused the other leaders of the Pack to shun me. They would no more listen to me than a random Werebadger."

"It seems your people here respect you greatly," he countered.

"Yes, but my people are far too few to get the Pack to change. There are leaders that would submit to you simply for being the Alpha, whether they agreed with you or not, while others will fight against giving up their standing over the rest."

Recognising potential enemies, he said, "Tell me about those that would fight back against that?"

She took a minute to ponder it, then said, "The leaders from Japan and Australia will likely submit purely on you being the Alpha, though both have similar feelings about the Five as I do. They only desire to not fight with the others, so they maintain an act of indifference towards them. The leaders from North America,

Western Europe, and Africa will all fight against your goal to make all equal. I must warn you, most of them will likely rebel against you simply because you were not born a Werewolf. They have gotten arrogant in time. The worst of them being the leader in England. It is her belief that since her father was the last Alpha, it is her right to rule."

"Has there ever been a hereditary title situation with the Alpha before?"

"No. It is not something that is passed down; you have to be born with the power of the Alpha, or you're simply not them."

"I realise this is a delicate, but curiosity demands I ask: has there ever been a female Alpha?"

Lisandra's face went suddenly sad, then said softly, "Once. She was the first Alpha we ever had. Not much has survived the time, but we do know that she was betrayed and murdered by those believing that even as an Alpha since she was a woman, she was inferior."

This news saddened Hyde as well, and given how obviously it pained Lisandra, he did not press for more information but resolved to learn more about her.

"Tell me more about this leader in England?"

"Daughter of a wealthy aristocrat. Spoiled and entitled but brilliant in business, if I am being completely honest. She isn't the "spoiled princess" type; she is ruthless and cunning, but her temper is fearsome when things do not go her way. She was the leader that helped Hitler rise to power in World War II, because the English monarchy refused to recognise her title."

Envisioning the countless unspeakable horrors that were perpetrated by the Third Reich and now finding that they had supernatural assistance was unsettling. He had always wondered how Hitler was able to last as long as he did against the Allies, but now this makes sense. Bembe had already explained to him that while the usual mythology of silver bullets was utter rubbish, Werewolves could be killed by severe trauma, that trauma being significantly more than the average human, however. So, an entire unit of Werewolf "super-soldiers" would explain a lot.

"Wait, Bembe had told me that the secret of our existence was the strictest law in all three of the Underkingdoms? How could she have helped the Nazis and not broken that?"

"She didn't bother hiding it. The Argentum Lupus are, unfortunately, the inspiration for Hitler's Wolf's Lair in Poland. The other leaders have always been intimidated by her and so no one sought to hold her accountable for breaking that law. And since they rarely left survivors, and those that did survive were considered mad on account of their reports of Werewolves on the battlefield, it was swept aside as a dark mark on our history. I have long wanted to bring her low for those actions alone, but, again, I lack the strength in numbers to do so."

Her clear frustration at being made so helpless against this "leader" from England made Hyde feel pity for Lisandra. He quickly squashed the emotion, however, feeling she would only be insulted by it. While he didn't assume she was easily insulted, pity in itself is not helpful to any situation and, therefore, not something she would value. Especially from one she is hoping will take control of the Pack someday. Instead, he decided to show her his intent.

"I will help you hold her accountable for her actions," he said with steel in his voice. "I am too new and too young to just take command of the Pack, but I will use my position to create unity within the council of Elders to ensure that everyone in the Pack will be treated fairly and justly. I know that to be Alpha is to be the ultimate leader, but to exclude and ignore the knowledge and experience of you Elders is a folly of epic proportions. It will take me centuries to even come close to what you have been through and know, and that is something the Pack can ill-afford."

Lisandra straightened and smiled warmly at him, then said, "I cannot say I am displeased with your choice. I have always felt that a singular ruler opened the group as a whole up to too much disarray, as how can one be attentive enough to watch the entire population?"

Hyde spent the next 18 months in this fashion, sparring and physically training with Bembe for a week, then mentally preparing with Lisandra for another week. His battle prowess continued to grow until the once one-sided victories became fewer and fewer. Eventually, Bembe could no longer best the stronger and faster Hyde despite his centuries of experience.

Equally, Lisandra felt that the young Alpha soaked up the knowledge she imparted to him better than she could have ever hoped for. He always continued to give her hope for a benevolent Alpha as he showed time and time again that he desired a democratic system rather than the outdated caste system that had brought so much turmoil to her people. She still studied him closely to ensure that he was not just telling her what he thought she wanted to hear, but his answers stayed consistently sincere.

It was finally time to introduce the Alpha to his new world properly.

[Chapter 9] — Grimlecht

October began with a cooler day than Hyde had grown accustomed to in this island life, and by cooler, it was only in the lower 80s compared to the sweltering 90 plus that was the norm. But more importantly, this marked the day that Lisandra had told him they would depart for Grimlecht finally. She said it was time to inform the rest of the Pack that an Alpha had arrived in this generation. The impending conflict with those seated in places of power unnerved the former schoolteacher. Up until this point, his only real experience with true conflict had been splitting up fighting children, hardly a precursor to potentially killing rivals.

"Given the dangers of the other Elders, do you think it wise for you to be there when I am introduced?" Hyde fretted at her.

"Backing you from afar would only hurt your position and ruin what little respect for me there is. No one can expect reward if unwilling to take the risk to achieve it." She responded coolly. She was obviously concerned but could ill afford to show it.

They climbed into the same car that brought Hyde to the villa those months ago, and travelled back to the same airstrip, though this time the Gulfstream sat there waiting for them. They boarded and prepared for the journey to first Lisbon to refuel, and then to Berlin, while the last bit to Grimlecht would be done by car.

While on the flight to Lisbon, they spent the time playing card games and actually visiting like old friends, but once the small jet left the tarmac to wing towards Berlin, the mood sobered, and there was very little talk. The tension on the aircraft was palpable as each knew that they were flying into a fight, to what severity was unknown, but a fight, nonetheless.

Given the potential conflict on the horizon, Lisandra ordered them to fly to the public airport. Far too many prying eyes for bloodshed was her reasoning, and to her credit, when they landed and taxied into the hangar, there were only airport personnel to greet them. Bembe had called ahead to a car service and there was a black armoured BMW X5 waiting for them. No driver was waiting, as they did not want one, as secrecy was key for the Werefolk capital. As the plane was finishing its taxiing into the hangar, they each quickly changed into winter-appropriate attire; they did not need the warmer clothing, but to lack them would have caused them to stand out quite a bit in the 10-degree Celsius evening. Lisandra stepped off in a dark grey Armani pantsuit and black 4-inch heels. Bembe opted for a matching grey John Phillip's of London suit but with an emerald-green turtleneck. Hyde decided to go with Armani as well but decided on a pure white suit with a jet-black dress shirt.

Bembe opened the door to the back for Lisandra and jumped behind the wheel of the luxury car after an attempt to open the door for Hyde was dismissed by the former's disapproving glare. Bembe had become Hyde's friend despite the disquieting nature of their meeting, and Hyde would not abide being waited upon as if he were some figure of royalty. As they sped out of the hangar, Lisandra started speaking.

"I cannot be sure who will be in the Capital at this time. Hopefully, the Baroness will not be visiting right now. We need time to get you introduced to the more hospitable ones first. If we can gain favour with enough of them, the rest would not dare to challenge you. Not enough of them would likely mean a civil war…

"At this point, we will try to stay optimistic. Step one will be introducing you to the German Elder. He is a fair but fierce man with somewhat of a hot temper. He will hear us out but to which side he will land is unknown. His distaste for his country's history and the Baroness's hand in that dark mark will give us an upper hand as he will likely sway in the opposite of her in virtually any decision she makes. Your decision to hold her accountable for those actions will also work well in your favour; he has long desired to bring her low for being a contributing factor in the Nazis gaining the power they did. Had it not been for her, he believes Germany could have kept Hitler from ever gaining the Chancellorship."

"I will make it a point to inform him of that desire then," Hyde said, forming somewhat of a plan in his mind on how to bring this Elder to his side.

"You have done well in not making it seem like you are only saying the things I *wanted* to hear; keep this up, and I do believe you can gain him as an ally. While there are many that will be needed, his support is pretty paramount." He nodded in agreement.

After driving north for a little over three hours, they entered Jasmund National Park. A short way past the entrance, there was an extra thick section of forest, though they stopped in the middle of it, and Bembe got out and spoke towards the wooded area. Suddenly, a rent appeared in the trees and bush, the whole scene splitting open as a secret gate is pulled back, revealing a green, single-lane tunnel of foliage leading away from the main road. Bembe returned to the car and steered it inside.

Admittedly, Hyde was getting a little exhilarated. He had only ever visited the States a few times but had always longed to see parts of Europe, Germany being high on that list. So, despite the fact that they were likely rolling into a political war, he was excited.

The tunnel of emerald trees was over a mile long, the ending showing a muted but brighter green as they approached it. As they passed back into the light, a large village sprawled out in front of them but was overshadowed by a thick covering of artificial trees, causing an impenetrable canopy, effectively hiding the city from anyone flying overhead. The denizens managed to meld the classic styles of architecture in a way that celebrated both the stones and stained glass of the Gothic and the tall arches of Romanesque, with a smattering of brightly coloured Bavarian-style chalets ringing the exterior.

As they pulled onto a cobblestone road, Bembe said, "The city is only 10 square kilometres but houses nearly thirty thousand Werefolk. Because of its location and the dense forest surrounding it, it has remained a secret this entire time. And since the forest and cliffs were made into a national park in 1990, we pushed hard for that legislation by the way, it has become even easier to keep it a secret."

Ever the teacher, Hyde said, "But wasn't there some Nazi resort being built here during the war?"

"The Colossus of Prora was several kilometres to the south, on the beach overlooking the bay. The Nazis never came up this far north by design," he finished with a wink in the rear-view mirror.

Hyde was staring out the window as they passed several people walking on the sidewalk, busily walking towards their countless tasks when from out of a shop strode a Werebadger. It, for he had no clue on its gender, stood approximately four foot tall, had a stocky frame, with strong arms and legs that each ended in a wickedly sharp claw, and was the traditional black and white of a European badger. Given its diminutive size, he could see how other Werefolk would find them weak. Unfortunately, since the dawn of time, small stature has always been seen as "weak" or "timid". Recalling with a smiling grimace his last two girlfriends, 5 foot 2 and 4 foot 11, respectively, he knew that "weak" and "timid" were words he would never even consider as adjectives for them. He knew better than to equate size to strength.

They drove almost a mile when the town centre came into view. The square was lined with shops and had many people and Werebadgers walking to and from the various businesses. There was a large, black, ornate marble fountain in the very centre that showcased all of the various Werefolk in their respective animal forms. As expected, the bottom of the fountain had a depiction of many Werebadgers, some standing while others were on all fours, holding up a ring that had Werefoxes sculking behind stone bushes that made up the main basin. Wereotters could be seen spraying water up into the next basin that depicted the Werecats in various positions of domestic bliss while one ear remained cocked to listen to the secrets of the world. The last stage before the Apex was a fluted column that showed scenes of the Werelynxes eliminating various historical figures of the humans: Julius Caesar, Mahatma Gandhi, Grigori Rasputin, and Henry IV of France, just to name a few. Standing above them all, in equally menacing positions, facing outward, were the three Apex predators comprising the ruling classes. Facing out towards the shops were the Ursa and the Manō hae, the former standing much taller than the latter.

They pulled the car between the fountain and a large stone edifice, the home of Tellus, and as Hyde stepped out facing the fountain, he looked up at the final part of the large fountain. Standing twenty or so feet above him was the statute for the

Argentum Lupus. Its menacing face snarling, claws outstretched to rake them across some unseen enemy. The pose and menace mirrored the other two statues on top of the fountain. This statue stood apart, though, for it was carved from pure white marble…

[Chapter 10] — The First Wolf

Lisandra joined Hyde in studying the imposing sculpture that adorned the entryway to the grand estate. "Tellus is the very first of us," she said, her voice a mix of reverence and caution. "He commands a lot of respect within the entire Pack, but Alphas have almost made it a personal point to make him feel inferior to them. While he honours the traditions of the Alphas, showing that you value his insight will go extremely far in gaining his favour. Thankfully, he is very progressive, so I believe he will listen to you openly, but he will carry old slights into the conversation. Living as long as we do, it is nearly impossible for us to let go of the past."

They turned as one to face the home of their first challenge. The large stone structure resembled a Gothic-era Catholic cathedral more than a home. The front of the massive building rose a hundred feet above them, with large solid oak doors that each easily stood twenty feet high. Tall stained-glass windows stretched towards the roof, depicting scenes important to the history of the Argentum. Battles raging between the Ursa and Argentum took precedence on the two large windows, while a depiction of the Eclipse that changed them all was shown on the circular window above the doors. Gargoyles snarled down at them from the roofline of the main building and the towers at each corner. What appeared to be a bell tower was lined with even more gargoyles glaring down from over two hundred and fifty feet above the cobblestones.

They walked up the smooth steps to the doors. Bembe was reaching for the massive door knocker hanging on the front when the door swung quietly inward. A tall, thin man in a tailored butler suit stood in the opening.

"Lady Lisandra, Lord Tellus is expecting you. Please follow me." He spoke English with a light French accent.

They said nothing but exchanged looks as they filed inside. Bembe had obviously been seen when they entered the forest, but Hyde and Lisandra had remained in the car, and the windows had been tinted too much to see inside. They scanned the long hall of the entryway for dangers but stayed closely behind the butler, who maintained a comfortable pace on the soft carpeted walkway. The inside was brightly lit thanks to the myriad of stained-glass windows throughout the structure, casting the interior in various colours.

The hallway ended after thirty feet, but the butler pulled up a short distance from two more oak doors. He turned to Hyde and asked, "May I get your name so that I may announce you properly, sir?"

"My name is Luther Hyde."

"And where do you hail from, sir?"

"Bermuda."

"Thank you, sir."

With that, he stepped forward one more pace, and the doors were pulled open inwards by unseen attendants. The grand hall beyond was breathtaking.

Black and white marble tiles covered the fifty by sixty-foot grand hall. Rich red velvet drapes hung on either side of each stained-glass window, and white marble comprised the walls themselves. Expansive gold and crystal chandeliers hung in every corner of the room, with an even larger and more ornate one hanging in the middle right in front of the raised dais that housed the large black marble seat with the lord of the house sitting upon it.

Lord Tellus wore a black pinstriped suit, and his long red hair was pulled back in a braid behind him in the style of a Renaissance aristocrat. His long, thick beard and bushy eyebrows framed shockingly purple irises that watched them with the piercing gaze of a hawk eyeing potential prey.

"May I present Lady Lisandra Castillo de Romero and her son, Bembe Vega de Castillo of Cuba. And, Luther Hyde, of Bermuda, your lordship," came the loud, clear voice of the butler.

"Thank you, Peter. Welcome, Lady Lisandra. You have come a long way for a visit. And I see you are still one for picking up strays," he spoke with a gentle German accent in a surprisingly soft voice. He was eyeing Hyde quite intensely as he mentioned "strays," though he stood when he saw the colour of Hyde's eyes. His purple gaze shot back to Lisandra as he said, "Have you found the next one?"

"I have, your lordship. But I should warn you, he is not the conventional type."

Immediately, Tellus's eyes narrowed in suspicion, "Explain."

"I have been tracking Luther since he was young, as he had the physical characteristics, but he did not change as he should have. It was then I realized he was not a Werewolf yet."

"Lady, you know the laws!" he said fiercely, grasping her meaning.

"I do, your lordship. I also know that our Pack is splintered to the point of being more vulnerable than we have ever been. Drastic changes needed to be made. As no one was willing to step up to do what is right, I did what was necessary for the good of the Pack."

"The law is not for you to decide whether or not you will abide by it! The Elders will not allow you to get away with this a second time. This will mean your death, Lisandra." He said this with a note of sadness in his voice, and Hyde decided to capitalise on this.

"Lady Lisandra will not be harmed for her actions," he said sternly, earning a surprised look from the ancient being. "Her intentions were pure, and law or no law, I will not have her punished for doing what is right."

"No one, not even the Alpha, is above the law. What hope do you have to rule your subjects if you flout the very laws of your predecessors?"

"Laws are a living thing, your lordship. One as old as you should surely see the benefit of laws evolving as time goes on."

"One does not exist for as long as I have by ignoring laws built to protect us," he spoke firmly, but his eyes softened.

"You make a valid point, Lord Tellus. But when those laws inhibit one from doing what is best for the Pack? Or rob us of a valuable member of our Pack for simply doing what she believes in? What then?

"We must take drastic steps to protect ourselves from every adversary, including ourselves. From my understanding of the Pack, as it stands right now, it is on the brink of total collapse. Infighting has caused rifts too wide to mend without a unifying force. I believe, with your help, I can make that a reality."

"You speak sweetly enough, and you seem sincere, but words are for children. Actions. Actions are the defining force in our world."

"Actions have always been louder than words; you are absolutely right about that. However, I must ask you, how much can be done with those in power actively working against that change? How much can be done and proven without aid from those in positions to do so?"

"Very little, if anything," he admitted.

"With that in mind, I have come to you for your aid, Lord Tellus. Not to supplant or further subjugate but to enact real change for the better of all. I do not believe this world needs any more dictators. What I believe it needs is someone willing to help correct things; the creation of unity within the council of Elders is that correction, I believe."

"A unity in the council of Elders has been tried, but it was mainly designed as a means of creating Werewolf 'royalty,'" he said. "A means to garner favour from those too strong to openly oppose. They are still in power. What are your plans for correcting this problem? For they will not willingly give up that power."

"I never wished to be a conqueror, but those that have been given power will be removed from it, and the Pack will decide who will be placed in these positions. If they refuse to give up that which they have not earned, they will be taken from their seat by my own hand."

"Ah… and you believe yourself capable of challenging those literally hundreds of years your senior?"

"I do—"

Hyde was cut off by Tellus leaping towards him, covering the distance faster than Bembe had ever hoped to have. In fact, he had moved so fast that he had already kicked Hyde in the chest before the others even realized he had moved from his seat. Hyde was thrown back by the sudden attack but landed, fully transformed in the brief moment he was airborne, on his feet. He centred his vision on the aggressor and watched as the Elder made his own transformation, doing so only a hair slower than himself. The old wolf stood nearly a foot shorter than Hyde's eight-foot height. Tellus sported a red pelt that had tinges of grey, his purple eyes blazing with fury. Hyde could not be sure what the intentions of the Elder were, but he was fully intending not to be a casualty of the First Wolf.

As Tellus had made the first move, Hyde felt obliged to return the gesture. He shot forward much as Tellus had and kicked the older wolf square in the chest, sending him across the room to slam against the far wall. He rushed over, intending to pin the Elder and perhaps determine why he was attacked, but by the time he got there, Tellus was already back on his feet.

The Elder swiped at Hyde with his right claw. Hyde slapped the attack away and returned the strike with a closed fist to Tellus's exposed left side, causing him to double over. While low, Tellus tried to bite at Hyde's legs, but the younger man was expecting it. Hyde sidestepped the teeth and swung his right knee into the side of Tellus's head, sending him sprawling.

Hyde turned, prepared to continue the fight, but Tellus was already getting back on his feet, a fierce grin on his face. The Elder launched himself at Hyde again, this time feinting a swipe to Hyde's left before spinning and aiming a powerful kick at his right. Hyde blocked the kick with his forearm, feeling the force of the blow vibrate through his bones, but he held his ground.

The two circled each other, testing defences and probing for weaknesses. Tellus lunged forward, but Hyde anticipated the move, stepping aside and using Tellus's momentum against him to throw the Elder across the room again. Tellus landed gracefully on his feet and came back at Hyde with renewed vigour. The fight continued, neither combatant aiming to truly harm the other but rather to gauge strength and skill. It was a dance of power and precision, each move calculated to test the other's resolve. Finally, Tellus leapt high into the air, aiming to bring both his fists down on Hyde in a hammer strike. Hyde met the attack head-on, catching Tellus's fists in his hands and pushing back with all his might.

For a moment, they were locked in a stalemate, muscles straining and eyes locked in a battle of wills. Then, slowly, Hyde began to push Tellus back. The Elder's eyes widened in surprise and grudging respect as he was forced to yield.

"Please forgive me, Milord," Tellus said, backing away with a hand up in resignation. "I have found that the best way to truly get to know someone and their intentions is to fight them. You reacted quickly to an attack, showing you are prepared even when you should not have to be. Your transformation was the fastest I have ever seen, faster than even mine. You showed both caution and courtesy when I did not arise quickly. I was hoping you were of lesser quality as I was planning on ambushing you when you got close. The caution shows that you recognize traps and do not attack recklessly. The courtesy shows one with honour. I do not know if you are the change we need, but I am willing to assist you and give you that opportunity to prove your words."

"Gratitude, First Wolf. I believe with your help, we can go further than any of us ever imagined."

[Chapter 11] — The Fated Pair

Bembe and Lisandra both took a deep breath to ease the tension that sprang to their muscles in light of the brief altercation. Neither of them knew what to expect, but in their wildest dreams, they never considered that Tellus would test Hyde in this fashion. Tellus was renowned for being hot-tempered, but he never lashed out physically, relying on his age and position to cow most before him.

"So, tell me what I can do to help," Tellus said as he slipped on a robe to cover his naked body. A servant appeared near Hyde's right side with a robe for him as well.

Lisandra spoke first, "You are helping now by accepting Hyde as the Alpha. With the First Wolf beside him, many of the would-be detractors will fall in line without further prompting. But you know there are still plenty of leaders that will denounce him simply for not being the pure blood they expect him to be."

Tellus nodded at this last part, "I, myself, do not find it favourable that he needed to be turned. But I find this to be minor, but I was never a big believer in "pure blood" at any rate. There have been many wolves that have been turned that proved to be far more gifted than those born as Argentum."

Lisandra also nodded at this as she recalled a young woman who had been turned. Turned in 1776, she gained notoriety in the Battle of Monmouth in 1778 for first carrying water to soldiers on the battlefield and then for manning a cannon after her husband was injured. History would name this woman "Molly Pitcher", but Lisandra knew her, to this day, in fact, as Mary Hays.

Hyde was focusing on the conversation intently, knowing that this meeting was of vital importance. A light draft blew across him suddenly, blowing a scent into his face and destroying any chance he had about focusing on anything else…

Involuntarily, his head turned towards the direction the draft and intoxicating scent came from, down a long hallway towards a large door that appeared to be slightly open. He was walking towards the door before his mind could even register that he was moving. The scent was cherry blossom, and it hit him with the force of a tidal wave. It drew him in and sent him to the calmest place he had ever been. Sweet and earthy notes collided with his mind, and the rest of the world melted away.

As he neared the door, those left in the grand hall were calling to him, but he could not hear them, so fixed was his focus. He looked through the door and came almost nose to nose with the most beautiful woman he had ever seen. Large topaz eyes stared back at him through the crack in the door, shining almost a light green from the light striking across them. Her face was framed with bright auburn hair that was curled and bounced playfully against her cheek. She was staring intently back at him, seemingly just as affected by his presence as he was by hers, and when she saw him fully, a smile crossed her full lips, and she turned her head to leave, giving him a devilishly playful look from the corner of her eyes before disappearing out a window nearby. He did not know who she was, but he knew in his soul he needed to meet her.

A rough hand on his shoulder yanked him out of the dream he had been entranced with. Spinning on the aggressor, he met a very angry-looking Tellus.

"You need to respect the privacy of even your subjects, Sire," his voice was heavy with disappointment and anger.

"I… I meant no disrespect, Lord Tellus. I smelled something, and curiosity consumed me."

"Consumed you? You were completely oblivious…" he came up short, a theory already forming in his mind. "Did it seem as though nothing else in the world existed? It was as if the scent was the centre of the universe, pulling you towards it?"

Bewildered that the old man could have so astutely guessed what had run through his mind, Hyde nodded slowly.

Bembe, not Tellus, responded, in a voice barely above a whisper, denoting this as a thing of vast importance, "The Fated Pair…"

"That is only a myth, I thought," Lisandra said, taken aback by the possibility.

"What is the fated pair?" asked Hyde, confused by the reverence displayed by the three wolves.

"Near the dawn of the Werefolk, an already ancient shaman had been consulted by families concerning the sudden and terrifying changes that were happening to their children, seeking answers from the only person they believed could offer them", Tellus began, "But even the wise man had no theories as to what happened nor why. He believed, however, that these new "children of the wild" would one day be the saving grace from an apocalypse. He foretold that "a great and powerful chieftain of the children of the wild with a silver streak in his mane would be the harbinger of salvation and pull the people of the world away from destruction". This foretelling is part of why Alphas became our leaders and why you are so treasured. What started as a belief strongly believed faded into obscurity once hundreds of years passed without damnation occurring.

"But the shaman also spoke of a pairing between two children of the wild that would usher in an era of either great prosperity or unescapable ruin. He did not know which was more likely, only that it was unavoidable. He had said, "it is the destiny of this fated pair to bring love and order to the land or to cast it forever in darkness", which the great many of us who believe in the foretelling believe that how the pair connects and feeds on one another will determine which way the story goes. If they are a good match, prosperity. Poor match… hell…

"The shaman said that the pair were so destined to meet that nothing could keep them apart. They would be drawn to one another, even without direct influence, but once near to one another, it would be as "if the world ceases to exist but for their heart of hearts".

Hyde was reeling from so much heavy information. He did not know how he felt about a "destined" partner, but he could not ignore the power this unnamed woman had on him. The knowledge that destiny states that he will either make the world a heaven or hell also did not sit well with him, no matter how strongly he felt for her, and he did feel strongly for her. As she was, undoubtedly, moving further away, he felt a great sense of loss getting stronger in him. He had had a girlfriend in college whom he had fallen in love with, and had been very happy with, but ultimately was not meant to be as he did not feel a long-term connection with her. He remembered the "honeymoon" period that every relationship started with and remembered he was head over heels for Cindy. But this feeling was diminished to a pale shadow in comparison to what looking into this woman's eyes was like. Just the breadth of time he had with her felt like a happiness that he could never even begin to imagine.

While a part of him rebelled against the idea of destiny dictating any part of his life, Hyde knew, without question, that he was going to find this woman.

Tellus opened the door wide to see who this destined partner was but only found an empty room with a window open, the curtains lightly dancing in the cool breeze blowing in. Having his suspicions, he ran across the plush office and swung the painting open, revealing the safe, slightly ajar.

Growling slightly, he said, "Fortunately, I may know how to find your mystery mate. Unfortunately, I will likely have to kill her…"

"What do you mean?" Hyde asked, still a bit distracted.

"She is likely part of the thieves guild, The Shifting Coin, and she has stolen something very precious to me."

Entering the room, Lisandra asked, "What did she take?"

"My ring."

[Chapter 12] — Leadership in Question

Luther was perplexed. The theft was always something to be abhorred, especially by the victims, but to react as though the loss was more than a minor annoyance did not make sense to him.

"Please forgive my ignorance, but while I sympathise with you on the loss of something you value, I don't see why this is quite as severe as you are making it out to be," Hyde said respectfully, but his voice still had the crack of disapproval to it.

It was Lisandra who answered, "A leader within the Pack changes; sometimes it takes centuries, other times… frequently. A leader's ring is a symbol to ensure that all others know that they are among the leaders, regardless of whether or not they actually know them. If it is stolen, the ring does not give the aura of leadership, but a leader lacking their ring is immediately excluded, the Pack assuming they lost their position. It was intended to make certain that no Pack member, new or old, could mistake with whom they were dealing. Please forgive me for asking, Lord Tellus, but why were you not wearing it?"

"It was always my intention to challenge Hyde when he arrived here, so I removed it to protect it from damage. A poor decision, apparently," Tellus was shaking his head in disgust with himself.

Hyde's mind began firing quickly as he digested this information. "So, despite the fact that he is the First Wolf, without his ring, the Pack will just assume he has lost his position of leadership and, therefore, no longer able to command the respect of those leaders we need to support us..." It was not a question but thinking aloud.

Tellus nodded in response, nevertheless. "That is why I am reacting to it so 'severely'", he said bitterly, not appreciating the reproach from the new wolf.

Abashed, Hyde said, "I apologise for my impatience, Lord Tellus. I see the need for severity and want to help retrieve your ring and status. What can I do?"

Again, it was Lisandra who answered, "We must go to The Shifting Coin and find this thief so we can try to recover his ring. Tellus, you should remain here for now."

"Why? Wouldn't it be better to have all the help we can get to get it," Hyde asked.

This time, Tellus responded, "Without my ring, every wolf from here to our destination will confront us in hopes of cowing me. I am very old and have made many enemies within the Pack, and while I can handle myself perfectly well, we do not need the delay, nor do we need the deaths of so many."

Hyde nodded slowly, seeing the truth in these words. "Very well. Wait here; you have my word that we will retrieve your ring."

[Chapter 13] — The Shifting Coin

"So, how are we going to find this thief?" Hyde asked as they walked out of the front doors of Tellus's home. He had donned some fresh clothes provided to him by the wealthy relic.

Bembe opened the driver's door and said, "Typically, the Shifting Coin is contracted by the Pack to steal items from the humans that are a danger to the Underkingdoms. Plans for weapons, intel on our various factions, things like that. Since we all interact with them frequently enough, there are contacts in pretty much every major city. We will try the one here, a rather overly confident Irish Werefox by the name of Lenox Toal. Our need of their kinds' services has given him a bit of an arrogance that will be difficult to deal with." He settled himself behind the wheel, and as Hyde clicked his seatbelt, stepped on the gas pedal, and roared the car towards the western side of the city.

Hyde considered his options and asked, "Arrogance can be a hurdle, but what about intimidating him?"

"Lenox has had a few centuries of wolves threatening him on a regular basis, so I don't think he can be pushed into giving us what we want," Lisandra said.

Hyde actually already considered this but needed the clarification. He had already come to understand the disdain his new community had for what many considered the "lesser" creatures amongst them. Knowing that he was also in his position for as long as he was, bribing the old thief wasn't likely to work either. An inkling of an idea sprang to mind.

"Given that the Underkingdoms treat the smaller predators as lower class, it is safe to assume that Lenox has reached his highest level within that organisation, yes?"

Lisandra turned to look at him out of the corner of her eye, "Technically, there is a rank higher than his rank of 'Facilitator', but, ironically, the thieves guild uses a democratic method for determining the Guild Master."

"Can we influence a vote in any way whatsoever? Offer to make him the Guild Master in exchange for his assistance?"

Lisandra and Bembe looked at each other, looks of consideration heavy on their faces. Bembe was the first to say, "It is possible. Normally, I would say a Pack leader endorsing a guild member would likely hurt their chances, but an endorsement from the new Alpha may be an entirely different possibility."

"Then we will play into his ego. That should make him a bit more amendable to our needs and get us further with his arrogant personality."

Bembe steered the BMW through the narrow streets and, after about ten minutes, pulled in front of a non-assuming brick building that reminded Hyde of older-style warehouses or factories. The building was built right on the river, and he suspected there was probably a water entrance that resembled the large wooden doors they currently faced. Bembe pulled directly in front of the doors, and seemingly of their own accord, they opened inward. Bembe slowly pulled the luxury car inside and put it in the park. He had barely let go of the parking brake when the vehicle was surrounded by twenty men, all holding a variety of submachine guns levelled directly at them. Above them, four more men ran out on to the catwalk holding rocket-propelled grenades and aimed those at the car. They all raised their hands and did not move another muscle as a lone man strode out on to the catwalk to stand between the men.

"Dia Daoibh", he said. "Now I know that shiny wagon is bullet-proof, but I am pretty sure it can't take these fireworks here. Go ahead and step out, and we'll have a wee chat."

Slowly, the three of them reached down and pulled the handle of their doors while keeping their free hands up and in plain view. Stepping out of the car and moving carefully, they turned to face the man, who must undoubtedly be Toal.

"Now, I know Ms Castillo de Romero and Mr Vega de Castillo, but I do not know you, sir. Though that silver streak in your hair does hint as to *what* you are. I am Lenox Toal, and you are?"

Taken aback by the willingness to be violent and yet shockingly polite, Hyde was thrown off his gameplan, likely the wily Werefox's goal.

With eyes circling the armed men around him, he said, "My name is Luther Hyde. And your assumption is correct about me. At least in terms of what I am. We did not come here for violence, though," he added quickly.

"Aye, I can tell that. But given your predecessors and the general attitude your kind has towards my kind, it seemed prudent to take measures," he said, though the weapons remained pointed at them. "So, since you're not here for a fight, what brings you to my door?"

"We have a p-" Lisandra started, but Toal cut her off.

"Please forgive me, Lady Lisandra. Interrupting is incredibly rude but given that the real power is the silver hair there, I'll be having his answer, not yours."

Having the brass cut off an Elder, even "politely", showed the true level of Toal's arrogance. He had to know that dismissing her in such a fashion would likely have severe reprisals. Hyde decided that despite himself, he liked this man.

"Never underestimate the power of an Elder, Mr Toal," Hyde warned, testing the waters a bit.

"Oh, I am quite aware of what the Latin Lady is capable of, and while that is formidable, here, I have certain... protections. Even from an Elder."

Confirmation of his suspicions.

"Powerful friends are always a boon to anyone of consequence, lifts their station quite nicely, wouldn't you agree?" Bait laid out...

A smile slowly spread across the face of the clever leader as the implication was understood.

"Aye, they do that indeed. But friends are only as good as they support you."

Fair, we all want to know that a new connection will be good for us.

"We were thinking of supporting you all the way to the top if you were willing to reciprocate..."

Eyes narrowed briefly. That's right, you smarmy bastard, you're not getting a lift without earning it.

"What do you have in mind?"

"For starters, how about simply lowering your guns? It's not exactly good manners to hold your friends at gunpoint while you visit."

He appeared to consider this for a moment before giving the slightest nod of his head. The weapons had the safeties flicked back on, and they were all lowered. He waved at them.

"Come on up to my office, and we can discuss how much more we can do for each other," polite and friendly, but Hyde could feel the tension was still there.

One of the men pointed to a set of stairs off to the right in the corner, and they walked up to the second floor, where Toal greeted them with a nod before leading them to a room on the opposite side of the catwalk. They walked into a plush and warm office that looked more like home in a castle than the cold, brick building that they had entered. Lenox noticed the curious look Luther was giving his office and gave a chuckle.

"A man's home should be his castle, aye?"

Hyde chuckled a bit himself and said, "Rarely do I see someone putting that saying to such exacting detail."

This made Lenox laugh even harder, finding some enjoyment in the wolf himself.

"When you have lived as long as I have, you learn that while *saying* something is nice, *doing* it is far more substantial for your own well-being."

"Fair point to you there."

"So, the new Alpha is an American, eh?"

Smiling at the common misconception, Hyde said, "Bermudian, actually."

"Well, if it isn't another islander fucked over by the English! Now I know you are someone with whom I can sit!" And the Irishman slapped him on the shoulder before going and sitting behind his large oak desk. He gestured for them all to have a seat.

"We have had a bit better luck with the English than the Irish have. We basically get just a mild neglect."

"Ah, I understand that. Now, let us dispense with pleasantries and small talk, shall we? What are you wanting from me, and why should I give it to you?"

"We need an introduction to one of your local thieves. Nothing negative or untoward, but it is vital. In return for your help with that, I am willing to offer something I do not believe you can get on your own."

A dangerous gleam sparked in the eye of the Werefox. Despite facing stronger predators, he had the courage and would not be insulted by anyone.

"And what, pray tell, is it that I want that I couldn't possibly get without your *noble* assistance, O great and powerful *Alpha*?"

Hyde recognised that Toal was trying to intimidate him. Whether it was intended to unnerve him or to make him slip, he was not sure. He decided to ignore it and continue as if Lenox had asked a basic question.

"The mastery of this guild," he said matter-of-factly.

Of all the things that Lenox could have thought the wolves would suggest, this was never even considered. Wolves, by their very nature, were arrogant and looked down on his kind, especially despite them being the closest in relation to one another than any of the other Werefolk. This Alpha had done the one thing he never could have imagined, he had unnerved him.

"There is an old Gaelic proverb that comes to mind: "an té is mó a gheallfaidh is lú a dhéanfaidh". It means, "he who promises most performs least". Your promise sounds sweet as honey, but a wolf's word doesn't mean much around here."

"I understand you have little reason to believe me, especially since I am a wolf, but surely there is something I can do to show you my word is solid."

Lenox looked intrigued by this, but his eyes searched their faces and the room for an answer. Typically, he would have told them to piss off, thinking nothing could make him trust a wolf. But what they offered was truly a heart's desire, so he forced himself to consider options that would allow this deal to go through. His eyes found a scrap of paper on his desk, a report he had been given two days prior of a situation he was unsure of how to handle on his own. This gave him an idea of what the young Alpha could do that would truly garner his trust.

"I'll tell you what, I have been dealing with an issue of one of your fringe Packs attacking my thieves and stealing their goods from them. To my knowledge, they are not sanctioned by an Elder, just young pups wanting to make their own mark and using the lack of care your kind gives us to their advantage. If you take care of these pups permanently, then we could make a deal. What say you?"

"How permanently?"

"Frankly, I don't care how you do it. Just ensure that they stop their activities against mine own."

Hyde almost breathed a sigh of relief. He wasn't afraid of meeting these young wolves in a fight, but he did not wish to kill anyone unless there was no other way.

"Then consider it done."

Lenox couldn't help himself; even despite the snub he felt he got earlier, he liked this young Alpha. Abruptly, he leaned forward and stuck out his hand. Wolves never shook hands with them; this would tell him plenty. To his surprise, Hyde reached out and firmly, not roughly, gripped his hand. They nodded their agreement, giving each other an approving nod.

[Chapter 14] — First Blood

With the location the wolves work out of in hand, Hyde and the others left the warehouse and sped towards the south side of the small city. Within just a few short minutes, they were in a very dark and somewhat dilapidated section of town.

Hyde was surprised when Lenox said the wolves worked out of this run-down part of town. He assumed that since wolves considered themselves "superior" to all others, they would have been bolder with their hideout. He supposed their lack of keeping its location a better-kept secret facilitated that emotion. Bembe had offered the rest of the explanation being that they were misbehaving in Tellus's own town, and those that misbehaved in an Elder's territory were subject to reprisals from that Elder.

The Shifting Coin Facilitator had told them that the minute pack was comprised of only seven to eight wolves, with the leader of sorts being an exceptionally arrogant bastard that went by the street name of Strike. He didn't know what Elder this "Strike" was beholden to, but he did have the theory that, despite the outward appearance of Elder support, this group was working in the area at the behest of a rival Elder in an attempt to embarrass the First Wolf. Lisandra gave the theory some validity by stating it had been tried in her own domain by a former Elder from North America. Only a very bloody battle between the two settled the conflict.

Sitting in the backseat of the car, Hyde wondered if he could find a peaceful solution to this problem. When someone was acting on their own behalf, reasonable solutions could be agreed upon. When someone is acting on the orders of someone else… well, it tends to stiffen one's resolve to their current course of action.

"Lisandra, do you believe that we can cow this upstart?" he asked her. "I really do not wish to fight this group and potentially kill any of them just to achieve our own means. Makes life seem a bit too disposable to me."

She considered her words carefully. She wanted to ensure that Hyde would do what was necessary but did not want to make him believe she was just some blood-lusting psychopath.

"I do believe that we can get the group to get back into line, but I do not believe we can achieve this with this Strike still alive. If he has garnered any loyalty or fear from his wolves, well then, they will just support whatever orders he gives, regardless of any influence we can get over them."

"That just confirmed my concerns," he said wearily.

Hyde was no pacifist. Even in his relatively peaceful life, he had recognised that no matter how unfortunate it may be, sometimes bloodshed was inevitable. He knew from personal experience that some men just could not be reasoned with; for some men, the only meaning was chaos. While he recognised the necessity of the action, he did not revel in the knowledge that very shortly, he was going to likely be ending a life.

They pulled into a neighbourhood of older, half-destroyed homes that were clearly from a time long past. Bembe pulled to the shoulder and parked the car.

"Are we ready for this?" he asked as he looked back at Hyde.

"We are not going in there," Hyde said. "Despite the numbers being against me, I think it will be best to show some strength and walk in there alone."

Bembe took a hurried breath, prepared to shoot this ludicrous idea down, but Lisandra cut him off.

"I feel this is a mistake. You are incredibly strong but against seven or eight wolves would be dangerous for even an Elder that has lived for centuries."

"I understand there is an extreme risk, but we cannot afford to give up this opportunity to show the rest of the Pack my strength. With the hurdles before us, if I cannot take down a few isolated wolves single-handedly, we will not be able to defeat the stronger enemies to come."

"You will not face them alone either, though," Bembe insisted. "You are too important to risk on this."

Hyde shook his head, "This is the proving ground I needed to cement myself as the Alpha. Many of the detractors will see me willingly facing this challenge solo and see the strength I possess, likely backing off with this show alone. Without this small fight, it may be a large battle that shows them I can lead; I would rather risk the lives of few than many. I go alone; these are my orders."

Neither of the older wolves liked this plan, but they would not go against a direct order from the Alpha, even one as young as him.

Secretly, each valued his desire to save lives, even while they believed this was the final time they would see him alive.

Without further words, Hyde stepped out of the car; a light but cold rain had begun to fall as he walked to the parking lot in front of the house the wolves used as a base. He walked down the centre of the road, ensuring he was in plain view the entire time. By the time he turned the corner into the parking lot, Strike was exiting the building with two wolves on either side of him.

The two wolves looked each other up and down, attempting to size the other up. To his credit, Strike looked around to rooftops and nooks and crannies of the street, showing he was cautious. His men had told him the man had come with two others but had not approached them.

"And who might you be?" a Slavic accent could be heard from Strike.

Hyde considered a multitude of introductions as he had made the walk to this confrontation. They had all seemed too much. Too arrogant, too polite, too threatening, too weak. He had landed on the only one that made sense as he entered the plateau of concrete.

"I am the Alpha."

If he had been intimidated at all, Strike did not show it. His entourage, however, looked immediately uncertain. They looked at one another behind their leader's back and even took a half-step backwards. Strike heard the movement, assumed their intentions, and growled, deep and low. They stopped moving but remained looking around uneasily.

"There is no Alpha right now. You do not fool me with that pretty hair dye, boy. But you have some nerve coming here and claiming that… what is your name? And what business do you have here?"

Hyde allowed a small smirk to turn the corner of his mouth up, showing the arrogant wolf his attempt to intimidate him had failed.

"My name is Luther Hyde. I am here to inform you that your actions against the Shifting Coin have come to an end. Return the items you have stolen and go back to whatever hole you crawled out of, or there will be consequences."

Of course, Strike had heard the rumours claiming an Alpha had risen once again. He dealt with information as well as stolen goods, so he knew everything that was important to hear. But as he had been born in between the times of the Alphas, he did not share in the fear and respect that most wolves had for the archaic title. Strike was not afraid of this man, even if he were the Alpha. So, he laughed. He laughed hard at the audacity this lone man showed. In between belts of laughter, he said:

"You may believe you are the Alpha; you may be just trying to frighten us. Either way, it makes no difference to me." His voice lost its mirth, and it deepened, "You do not frighten me, and I will not do as you say."

As his words faded, a wolf stepped out of the shadows behind Hyde and stepped in close, breathing hot breath down his neck. Hyde had smelled the wolf long before it moved, so he did not react as the group had anticipated he would, instead opting to spin suddenly and punch the wolf in the throat; he then followed the spin around and faced Strike once again. The shock of the speed and the force behind the punch caused the wolf to crumple, desperately trying to gain its breath again.

Now, there was a note of fear behind Strike's eyes. He did not know if this enemy, for an enemy he clearly was, was an *Alpha* exactly, but he was powerful. Much more powerful than he previously considered him. Inner conflict roiled inside him. On one hand, he had his orders, and she was not one to move against. But on the other hand, this was definitely an enemy not to be trifled with. His fear of the unknown outweighed his fear of the unknown, however, and he began changing.

He reached to his shoulder and ripped his shirt and jacket off as the fur sprouted from his skin. He grew taller as the bones in his ankle shifted up, his elongated foot now lifting out of the boots he wore, the claws growing from his toes shredding the fronts of the boots. His legs grew in girth, ripping the grey cargo pants he had on. He bent down at the waist, allowing his growing spine easier movement. His ears grew longer as his small tail fell out behind him. He then threw up his arms, extended his body to its full height of seven feet, and let loose a rage-filled howl to the insolent man before him.

Hyde patiently waited for Strike to shift, in fact looking almost bored at the wait. This unperturbed demeanour threw off Strike's guards fully. They knew that they were to shift as well and support their leader, but an enemy that presented that level of indifference was an entirely different beast altogether, and they took more steps back. Strike was unaware of any of this, but it would not matter to him anyway; he was committed to the cause at this point. He rushed forward.

Again, Hyde stood very calmly and waited for the raging and rushing wolf to reach him. It was as if time slowed to a crawl. Hyde even took his eyes off of Strike long enough to double check that his guards were keeping to their places, furthering the feelings of sheer panic in the two. Strike did see this, and his nerve cracked even further in that split second. But again, it was too late. He reached his claws toward Hyde with the intent of slicing him across the chest. His claws found nothing but air however, Hyde moving out of the path with a sliver of a second left to impact. Hyde had lowered down on his right knee while stepping his left leg out to his left, planting the foot, and taking his weight before lunging forward and extending his right fist into Strike's stomach. Hyde was aiming for Strike's spine and put all of his considerable strength into the hit. The combination of the forward momentum of Strike's charge and the ferocity of Hyde's punch caused several organs to rupture from the impact. Before either of them knew it, Strike had made his final move on this plane of existence. Strike had long enough to step away from Hyde, look at him one final time, then collapse at his feet.

Hyde was still looking at Strike's body as he slowly, methodically straightened back up, smoothed the front of his coat, and pulled his cuffs back down to his wrists. Then he looked at the remaining wolves from the tops of his eyes through his hair.

"Does anyone else wish to maintain this course of action?" his voice was calm. It was as if he had just sat on a park bench on a warm summer day. This made him seem even more terrifying to the small gang, the rest of whom were stepping out of the house to get a better view of what had just transpired. They looked at one another, then as one, slowly shook their heads.

"I want to know who got you to betray your own like this…" It was not a question.

None of the gang members really wanted to be a snitch, but this being had killed their leader in one punch, and none of them wanted to see what else this man would do. So, one of their newest members answered from the back:

"Th-th-the Baroness said if we made Tellus look like he couldn't control his region, she'd give us his ring when she took over. We would just have to answer to her."

"Do you have the ring?"

"Y-y-y-yes, Sire. And the thief that we hired."

"Why do you have her if she completed the contract you hired her for?"

"Strike didn't want to pay her."

"I feel like you have all lived without honour long enough… I need a volunteer to take me to the thief and retrieve the ring."

The same youth that had been speaking slowly raised his hand. As Hyde walked towards the building, the wolves parting before him, he said:

"The rest of you are to present yourselves before Lord Tellus and confess your transgressions to him. I have your scents; if you do not follow these orders, I will find you, and you already know what I am capable of doing to you…"

Like mists in the morning sun, the wolves dissolved into the night, each moving quickly to do as they were told. A couple ran past Bembe and Lisandra, hung their heads in shame and ran faster. The two older wolves ran towards the house to see what had happened, first witnessing the body of the broken former leader of the thieving gang on the pavement, then seeing Hyde stride out of the house carrying a woman in his arms.

At that moment, they realised he had been right. Despite their already steadfast loyalty to him, they both felt a profound sense of awe in this man. His clothes were not even dirty or torn, so he had managed to kill a fully shifted Werewolf without shifting himself, and he had done so without any real difficulty. He truly was the Alpha.

[Chapter 15] — Lexie

Some things cannot be explained or even understood if one has never experienced them. True and primal fear is one of those things. Sure, one can explain intellectually all day long the concepts and theories of fear, but to truly understand it, one has to *feel* it. Fear changes you. Moulds you into the creature it can feed on if you let it.

So, when Lexie opened her eyes and saw yet another man sitting near her, her reaction was immediate and brutal…

Hyde was sitting silent vigil by the resting woman's bed, contemplating what was the next move. They had driven to a small inn Lisandra knew to sort out that move. He knew that he had accomplished the goal of gaining Lenox's assistance, but he was certain that Tellus was going to want blood for this woman's actions. Blood Hyde was quite committed to denying him already.

He was in the middle of forming an argument to make to the First Wolf when the hit occurred. Without warning or hint of her being alert, she had lashed out with a savage kick to his head, sprawling the powerful wolf as though he was made of so much kindling. With superhuman speed, he recovered to his knee, but even this was too slow as a red fur-covered knee sprang to his nose, smashing the soft cartilage to his skull, sending sparks and intense pain rippling through his face. He blindly struck out with a weak left-handed swipe, an attempt to push back the attacker, whom he suspected was the battered woman who had spent the night passed out in the bed but still was not entirely sure, so swift the attack had been. This movement only served to put his forearm in a convenient position to be bitten hard. The searing, white-hot pain shot through him, causing the sudden burst of adrenaline to send lightning through his body, spurring the rapid change from mild-looking high school teacher Luther Hyde into the massive eight-foot behemoth Alpha he was now. Using his new height and additional strength, Hyde reached out and gripped his attacker by the throat, pinning her silver-furred body to the wall, for it was the thief he had rescued that had attacked him.

His primal fury could not be sated by merely stopping the onslaught, so it caused a deep, rumbling growl to emerge as he spoke:

"I know you have been hurt by those wolves, and I know your first instinct is to kill any wolf that stands before you, but" he softened his voice as best he could give the rage she had caused, "I am not your enemy." He loosened his grip and backed up. "I am not with those wolves. In fact, I pulled you from their den and killed their leader."

Lexie bent forward slightly, working to catch her breath, both from the exertion the quick fight had put on her weakened body and also from the surprise she had gotten from this truly enormous wolf pinning her helplessly against the wall. He had gripped her throat but had not cut off her breathing, merely a show of strength, a squeezing that shockingly sent shivers through her. Despite herself, she had gotten excited over this display of gentle dominance. She was still wary of this stranger, for she was no fool, but in showing that he could exert his will so deftly, he had shown her that he truly meant her no ill will. It was obvious he was strong enough to end her easily if he had wished it.

Still trembling somewhat, she said, "I am sorry. I just saw another man and thought you were going to hurt me like… he had."

Feeling the tension ebbing from the room, Hyde was able to better control the anger in his voice and was able to speak soothingly now, "I understand that. I am sorry for the suffering you have dealt upon you from my species. May we return to human form and discuss things from a less threatening standpoint?"

Without waiting for her reply and wishing to show his wish for peace, Hyde began changing back. Within seconds he was human once again, feeling pleased that he had been able to diffuse the situation from getting any further out of hand. His pleased feeling faded rather quickly when he noticed her gaze wandering south of his waist and shoot off with an approximation of blush for a silver fox's face, and he became acutely aware that he changed right into a nude form before this beautiful woman.

"So, I uh- will step out to give you some privacy and to uh- go and uh- make myself a bit less uh- "he looked down, beyond the blissful realm of embarrassment as he noticed his member betrayed just how exciting the quick fight had been for him. Without another word, he rushed from the room to hopefully die in another.

Alas, death did not come to him, and he walked to his room down the hall. As he walked past the adjoining hallway, he saw a very bewildered Bembe standing there, clearly having heard and likely responding to the commotion that had come from her room. His bewilderment quickly melted to uproarious laughter once he noticed the same betrayal Luther had noticed in the room.

"Oh… fuck off, smartass…" Luther muttered.

Bembe turned and howled with laughter as he exited the second floor, turning on the stairs to look at him again, only to be redoubled in his mirth at the situation.

At first Luther's rage reasserted itself as he never did enjoy being the brunt of someone's entertainment, but it quickly dissipated as he considered the man's point of view. Once he put himself in Bembe's shoes, he could not help but chuckle at his own predicament. Rolling his eyes and chuckling to himself, he resumed walking to his room, nevertheless praying no one else would bear witness to his walk of shame.

Lexie had been watching surreptitiously from her doorway upon the scene of these two obvious friends' interaction, partially to see if the man truly was the peaceful man he wanted her to believe, partially because she enjoyed his visage and wished to see it more. Upon seeing his smile at his own awkwardness, warm and beaming with the honesty of believed internal aloneness, she easily believed he was the peace-seeking wolf he claimed to be. For how could one lie to themselves, even if they had been lying to her? She shot one last appreciative glance at his ass before blushing to herself and closing the door.

Hyde took his time getting dressed, assuming the young woman was wishing for a shower after her ordeal. He waited in his room, gathering his thoughts in regard to this Werefox and her effect on him. He knew he was inexplicably attracted to her, but why had a life-or-death struggle with her caused him to become so aroused? He considered what he knew of wolf mating rituals, as this was his only real frame of reference, and remembered that wolves sometimes act aggressively during their mating to assert their dominance over their potential mate. He supposed the aspect likely was true for Werewolves, though it did nothing to assuage his embarrassment at becoming so fully erect in front of her. He did not even know her as of yet. He shook the thoughts from his head for the time being; however, he had plenty of time to grapple with those implications later. He had been reeling from the embarrassment for over fifteen minutes by this time, assuming her bathing to be complete by now.

A few more minutes passed by as he continued to calm his thoughts and nerves before he returned to her door and knocked on it lightly, a welcoming voice allowing entrance, and he opened the door.

She had gotten dressed in the clothes Lisandra had laid out for her the night before. She wore the black wool pants over some three-inch black heels and a simple but wonderful black cashmere sweater. She was now sitting on the other chair in the room, the chair he had been sitting in when she waylaid him, now pulled in front of her own.

"I assumed a more civilised discussion would include sitting face to face as equals," she said coolly to him. She was determined to show she meant no ill will as well at this point.

"I agree," he responded as he took his seat, his eyes never leaving hers during his entire movement from the door to his seat.

"So, I'd imagine your first question would be, where is the ring?"

"Actually, no, we retrieved the ring from Strike already. Our biggest and most vital question is if you know *who* Strike's master was and *why* you were hired to steal the ring, to begin with."

"Strike didn't give me a reason why he wanted the ring. I had asked him when we had our meeting, but he said it wasn't important for me to know. As to the "who", I only can assume it was the Baroness."

"Why would you assume that?"

She sighed heavily at this, "Because I overheard Strike telling his guys that 'the Baroness doesn't want any witnesses'. I had told him, cos I'm an idiot, that you had seen me at Tellus's home before I could get away. As soon as I had told him that, he hit me-" the reliving of the ordeal weighing on her heavily "-and he kept hitting me until I lost consciousness at some point. When I woke up, that's when I heard him talking about the Baroness. I thought he was going to kill me right then, but-" she began breathing quickly.

"That's okay. You don't have to tell me more than that. I don't want to make you relive it any more than I have already."

He reached up a hand to her shoulder, a gesture meant to comfort, but she immediately flinched out of reach; he snatched his hand back as if he had unintentionally burned her with it.

Knowing what she endured to put that flinch in her caused his blood to boil anew. He wished Strike were alive only so he could end him more brutally and creatively the second time around.

"I'm going to go and let you get some rest. No one will bother you, nor will they try to stop you if you should want to leave. I urge you to stay, though. Tellus is severely pissed over the theft, and I would very much rather talk to him before he meets you himself."

She could not bring herself to speak, so she only nodded, her eyes drawn to the floor, the nightmare of the last day swimming before her eyes. She felt what little calmness she felt leave at the sound of the closing door.

[Chapter 16] — Killer in the Dark

As Hyde walked into the sitting room of the safe house, Bembe was finishing up a call. Lisandra stood up from her seat and walked over to him with Bembe.

"How is she doing?" Lisandra asked.

"She's… scarred but well," was all Hyde could think to say. Wishing to move away from the angering thoughts of Lexie's experience, he turned to Bembe and asked, "Was that Lenox?"

"Yes," Bembe answered. "He understands that she may need some time to rest, given what was done to her, but he will only believe she is alive by seeing her for himself. He won't just trust our word."

"Frankly, if I were him, I wouldn't either. Wolves are not proving to be the most trustworthy out of the Werefolk."

Lisandra spoke then, "Now you see the need for a strong leader to take control. We need someone that can help return us to honour."

"There seems to be a lot of bad habits needing to be cut out before we can do that," he responded. To Bembe, he said, "Will he be willing to come here to verify her safety? I do not know if she is willing to travel even just across town, but I do not even wish to ask her to decide right now. She is free to make her own decisions, of course, but I just don't want to push her to do something purely for our own means."

"I asked him this already, and he is willing, but only if you will come to him yourself and escort him here. As a show of faith, he said."

"I don't see any other choice short of putting it on her. I will go now. Lisandra, will you let her know that I am going to go get Lenox and bring him here?"

She nodded, "Yes, of course."

A short while later saw Hyde pulling the sleek car in front of the warehouse once again. This time, the doors opened immediately, and he drove in slowly. Thankfully, this time was sans the ring of death-dealing guards and only Lenox with two guards waiting for him.

"Greetings, my friend!" Lenox was in high spirits.

"Hello, Lenox. You seem quite pleased."

"Well, not only did your man, Bembe, call to inform me of Lexie's safe rescue from the clutches of those villains, but men I pay well to be trustworthy have reported the same. This visual check is mainly a formality. I hope you understand."

"I do. And I am pleased you have heard it from your own men. Trust is a hard-earned commodity when so much treachery has been the norm."

"Ha! Too true, my frie-"

A gunshot from behind Hyde rang out, cutting Lenox off as a bullet ripped through the Werefox's upper right shoulder. With all of the speed his enhanced body could muster, Hyde sprang forward, grasping Lenox and carrying the stunned Irishman with him as he dove behind some crates to cover.

Lenox was sputtering, clearly infuriated but confused, as he yelled, "Wha- what is this?! Treachery of your own?!"

More shots were ringing out as one of Lenox's guards fell to the concrete floor to never move again, while the other guard shot out blindly in the direction of the attacker's shots and moved towards cover of his own. He was a step from cover when a well-placed shot through his forehead spat his brain matter on the wall behind him.

"This isn't me. Where are the rest of your guards?"

"I wasn't expecting an attack, so I sent them off to do their usual runs!"

"So, we don't have any backup here?!"

Dejectedly, Lenox hung his head and muttered, "No."

Hyde carefully peeked one eye around the crate to see if he could spot the assailant; a shot splintered the wood near his eye. He ducked back down just as another bullet ripped through the space his eye was just occupying.

Anger swelled inside Hyde at this cowardly attack from the dark. It raged within him until he decided to give in to white-hot fury, and his wolf form tore itself into the fight. Still crouching behind the crates, Hyde turned to a more than slightly terrified Lenox.

"Stay in cover. Are you armed?"

Lenox pulled a Walther PPK from a shoulder holster and nodded. With the belief that Lenox had his own back, Hyde leapt straight up into the rafters some forty feet above them. He gripped the steel I-beam that held the roof aloft and, clambering hand over hand, made his way towards the dirty glass panel above where the shooter had been. He tried to look through it and determine who was shooting, but the glass was too filthy to make out any details but a shadow. Hyde zeroed in on the shadow and, going for broke, launched his massive self through the glass directly at the would-be assassin.

The sudden explosive shattering of glass came as a complete shock to the gunman, as he had been busy reloading when Hyde made his jump into the rafters, not seeing the blur of white-grey fur flying into the air. He had just been sighting in to rain more lead on the area when the eight-foot Werewolf came through the glass wall above him like mother nature's wrath. He lifted the 9mm Baretta more in surprise protection of his face than an actual attempt to shoot. But even in this task, he failed, as Hyde landed on him and pinned him with grips of pure iron, holding his wrists to the ground above him, his gleaming white teeth a mere inch from the killer's face.

Knowing his next breath could very well be his last, the killer immediately turned into his own form, that of a Werelynx, and lashed out with his foot claws at the belly of Hyde. One foot missed, barely scratching Hyde's side; the other met with full purchase, and the Werelynx sank all five claws into Hyde's stomach and tried to tear down towards his waist to maximise the damage. Hyde instead had let go of one wrist and, with his free hand, grabbed the ankle of the attacker and wrenched up, tearing the claws out of his flesh with the horrid sound of ripping skin and muscle. With a free hand now, the assassin lashed out at Hyde's face, looking to ruin his eye and get away once he was half-blind. This plan was thwarted by the ever-faster Hyde, who pulled back in time to save his eye but not his muzzle, which was raked savagely by the claws of the killer. While he missed his target, the lynx used the small measure of distance he had made himself to use both feet to climb and flip over under Hyde, twisting and breaking his own arm in the process, winning his freedom and attempting to dart out of reach.

The lynx, again, misjudged the speed and reflexes of the great wolf, who then swiped out a clawed hand, slicing the belly and chest of the lynx wide open, spraying crimson all over the paving stones before him. Enraged, the lynx sprang on top of Hyde and bit deep into his neck, trying to sever his spine with his strong jaws. Any other wolf would have been taken down with such a tactic, but Hyde was larger, muscles thicker, and kept the lynx's short teeth from reaching the fatal area. Despite being saved from death thanks to his unique physique, Hyde was not going to allow this attempt on his life to go unanswered, jumping high into the air before leaning back as far as he could to ensure when he returned to earth, he would land on his back, and crush the diminutive killer beneath him.

The lynx saw the goal and released, pushing off just in time to survive the fall, but not enough to avoid having his right leg trapped under Hyde and having it break in five places. He was done. Innards spilt out from the tear in his belly, leg broken to the point that he could not even hobble away; the lynx knew he had been bested. He continued to try and pull himself away by his arms as Hyde got back on his feet, taking a second to recover from the hard hit to his back. When Hyde rounded on the lynx, however, the lynx looked back at him defiantly, spit at him, then reached to his own throat and ripped away his own skin, muscle, and veins. His life spraying all over the ground in front of him, within a hairsbreadth of a second, dying before the Alpha.

Though he was shocked to his very core, not believing someone would be willing to kill themselves so brutally rather than speak, Hyde dragged the gore-streaked corpse back inside the warehouse to where Lenox had been staying in cover. Once he stepped around the crate, he found the Werefox clutching his smoking weapon but pointing in the opposite direction as the fight had been in.

"He had a partner with him," was all Lenox said when Hyde asked what happened.

Hyde walked over in the direction Lenox was facing and found a young Werelynx gasping slightly, air bubbles forming above the holes in his shirt where the thief had shot him. They locked eyes for the briefest of moments before the life drained from the scared creature's eyes. The look that remained on the smaller Werefolk shook Hyde to his core. He was a teacher, damn it! Why was he now party to the killing of others…

[Chapter 17] — An Elder's Dilemma

Meanwhile, in his sprawling estate, Lord Tellus sat deep in contemplation. The grand hall, adorned with ancient tapestries and relics of the Pack's storied past, felt suffocating as he mulled over his predicament. He knew that ambition ran rampant within the Pack, but the audacity to seize power so openly was what troubled him most now. The Baroness had already shown her lack of morals and respect; her collaboration with the Nazis in the 1940s was a testament to that. Yet, Tellus had always believed that even she would not risk the wrath of the First Wolf.

Tellus's position was one of honour, revered by those who saw him as the First Wolf, a mythical figure of their lineage. However, this reverence did not translate into actual power. His command was spiritual, not political. He had no influence over the Pack's decisions as a whole, a fact he had presumed would shield him from internal strife. He had clearly been mistaken.

The recent developments forced Tellus to consider the unthinkable: an all-out war against the Baroness's forces. The mere thought of spilling the blood of his own Pack mates for the sake of their overzealous leader was abhorrent to the old one. Yet, the idea of targeting the Baroness directly presented its own moral quandaries. Assassinating one of his own kind violated his deepest principles, principles that had guided him for centuries.

His position had recently been bolstered by the backing of the Alpha, a development that brought both hope and new challenges. The Alpha's support demonstrated his influence but also highlighted potential adversaries. Many within the Pack openly opposed the idea of a Turned Alpha, viewing it as a break from tradition. But Tellus knew that Luther was no ordinary Alpha. From their first encounter, it was evident that Luther possessed a natural leadership that could unite the Pack.

Tellus watched Luther closely during the initial trials, noting his strength, wisdom, and strategic mind. Luther's capacity for compromise struck Tellus as a perfect tool to showcase his leadership to the Pack. Those who revered power would see Luther's strength and wisdom, and their numbers would swell.

The grand hall's oppressive silence was interrupted by a soft knock. A young servant entered, bowing deeply before speaking. "Lord Tellus, the Alpha is here to see you."

"Send him in," Tellus replied, his voice a mix of weariness and resolve.

Luther entered, his presence commanding and reassuring. He moved with the grace of a predator, eyes sharp and calculating. "Lord Tellus," he greeted, bowing slightly, a sign of respect and solidarity.

"Luther," Tellus acknowledged, gesturing for him to sit. "We have much to discuss."

Luther sat across from Lord Tellus, his tone modest yet resolute as he recounted the confrontation. "It wasn't a fair fight, Lord

Tellus," he admitted, rubbing his knuckles absently as if feeling the impact all over again. "Strike was quick, young, and clearly devoted to the Baroness's cause. But he was also reckless, too eager to finish things fast. I saw an opening, and I struck him… harder than I intended. It was over in a single blow. He went down and didn't get back up. I wish it hadn't come to that. I was prepared for a prolonged fight, but his overconfidence left him vulnerable. I didn't want to kill him that way, but he left me no other option. I hope his death, as swift as it was, will serve as a warning to the Baroness and her followers."

Luther paused, his gaze softening. "Afterward, I found Lexie, the thief who stole your ring. She was tied up and wounded, caught in the crossfire of a plan she never truly belonged to. When she finally had a chance to explain, she revealed that the theft wasn't her idea; she was forced into it by Strike, who was acting on the Baroness's orders. The entire plot was designed to make you look weak, but Lexie… she's not the villain here. I've spoken with her, and I believe she was coerced, driven by fear rather than malice. I entreat you, Lord Tellus—please, show her mercy. She's a pawn in a larger game, not the architect of our troubles. If we're to stand for justice, we must also stand for understanding."

The two leaders sat across from each other, the weight of their conversation hanging heavy in the air. Lord Tellus sat in silent contemplation for a moment, his stern face etched with the lines of deep thought. Finally, he sighed, the weight of the situation settling heavily on his shoulders. "I will forgive her, Luther," he said slowly, each word filled with a reluctant yet genuine sincerity. "If what you say is true, then Lexie is more a victim than an accomplice, ensnared by the Baroness's schemes rather than driven by malice of her own. I'll grant her clemency, but know that my trust is not given easily nor fully restored with mere words." He paused, his gaze darkening. "This recent plot only further proves the lengths to which the

Baroness will go. Her cruelty is growing more desperate, more calculated. We must be ready, Luther. If she's willing to weaken us from within, then there's no telling what she will attempt next. We can't afford any more missteps—our survival depends on it."

Luther nodded his expression grave. "She seeks power at any cost, disregarding our traditions and the lives of our brethren. We must act, but we must do so wisely."

Tellus appreciated Luther's measured approach. "An open war would decimate us," he said. "But targeting her directly poses its own challenges. We must find a way to undermine her without betraying our principles."

A thoughtful silence followed, each lost in their own contemplation. Finally, Luther spoke. "We must reveal her true nature to the Pack. Show them the extent of her betrayal and the danger she represents. If we can unite the Pack against her, we can isolate and neutralize her without resorting to widespread bloodshed."

Tellus nodded slowly, the plan taking shape in his mind. "Yes, we must expose her. Gather evidence of her atrocities and present it to the Council. Let them see her for what she truly is."

Luther's eyes gleamed with determination. "I will need your help to gather this evidence. Your knowledge and connections within the Pack are invaluable."

"Of course," Tellus agreed. "We must move swiftly and decisively. The Baroness's influence grows with each passing day. We cannot afford to wait."

As they planned their next steps, Tellus felt a renewed sense of purpose. With Luther by his side, he believed they could overcome this threat. The Alpha's strength and wisdom were the key to uniting the Pack and restoring balance.

Together, they would expose the Baroness and her treachery, securing a future where the Pack could thrive in unity and peace. Tellus knew that this was only the beginning of their struggle, but with Luther leading the way, he felt a glimmer of hope for the first time in years.

[Chapter 18] — The Baroness

The pivotal moment had arrived. Luther Hyde and his group were set to meet with the current Council of Elders. Despite all the preparation, Hyde felt a surge of trepidation, much like the days leading up to this event. He knew what must be done and still believed it was the best option to bring peace, not only to the Pack but to himself. Hyde had spent most of his life in the middle of everything, never showing too much commitment to one side or the other, preferring compromise. Yet, in this matter, he knew he must choose a side. To achieve peace, he had to step forward and accept his new responsibility. However, his lifelong struggle with self-esteem sought to undermine his choice, tempting him to bow before the Baroness.

Despite his lack of confidence, Hyde had a firm grasp of right and wrong, and he knew the Baroness was wholly wrong. He had heard much about the offspring of his predecessor—their entitlement, vanity, cruelty, and outright evil. Hyde knew better than to take anything at face value. Given what was needed to solidify his command of the Pack, he required proof of the Baroness's malevolence. Determined to find this proof on his own, he requested time alone and drove from Grimlecht to Berlin, heading to the Deutsches Historisches Museum.

Upon arrival, Hyde delved into the museum's archives, seeking historical records that could shed light on the Baroness's actions. He began with "Dark Prophecies: Hitler's Obsession with the Occult" by Dr Evelyn Whitaker, a comprehensive exploration of the Third Reich's occult involvements. The book painted a chilling picture.

In the dimly lit study of the Berghof, Adolf Hitler sat engrossed in ancient texts and occult manuscripts. His obsession with uncovering supernatural powers that he believed could secure his dominance over the world had led him down a perilous path. Among these texts, one name kept recurring: the Baroness. Known only by this enigmatic title, she was reputed to possess arcane knowledge and mystical artefacts said to hold immense power. More intriguingly, she was a Werewolf, capable of transforming at will, unbound by the cycles of the moon.

Rumours of the Baroness circulated within esoteric circles for years. Some claimed she was a direct descendant of the infamous Countess Elizabeth Báthory, while others whispered that she had made a pact with otherworldly entities. Her true identity was shrouded in mystery, and her whereabouts were known to only a select few. Hitler's sources, however, had pinpointed her current residence—a secluded château in the Black Forest.

Determined to meet this enigmatic figure, Hitler dispatched a small, elite team of SS officers led by Heinrich Himmler to negotiate an audience with the Baroness. Himmler, himself deeply entrenched in the occult, was both excited and apprehensive about this mission. The journey to the Baroness's château was fraught with challenges as if the very forest conspired to keep intruders at bay. After days of treacherous travel, Himmler and his team finally arrived at the imposing gates of the château.

The Baroness was a striking figure dressed in a flowing black gown that seemed to absorb the light around her. Her eyes, an unsettling shade of crimson, held a knowledge that transcended the ages. She welcomed Himmler with an eerie grace, her voice a soft, melodic whisper that seemed to echo through the cavernous halls of her home. Himmler presented Hitler's request for her assistance in acquiring occult artefacts and harnessing supernatural powers. The Baroness listened intently, her expression inscrutable. After a long silence, she agreed to share her knowledge—but at a price. She demanded complete autonomy within the Third Reich and a guarantee that her secrets would remain safeguarded.

Over the next few months, the Baroness became a shadowy figure within the upper echelons of the Nazi regime. She provided Hitler with ancient relics and performed arcane rituals that she claimed would enhance his power. Her influence over Hitler grew, and soon she became an indispensable advisor, her counsel sought on matters both mundane and mystical.

The Baroness did not come alone. She brought with her a loyal group of Werewolves, each capable of changing form at will. This group was a fringe faction of a much larger entity known only as the Pack. The Pack's existence was known to few, even among those deeply involved in the occult. It was said to be a vast and ancient network of Werewolves spread across Europe, each cell operating independently but united by a shared purpose and a secretive code of loyalty.

Hitler and his inner circle were fully aware of the Baroness's nature and her allegiance. They saw in her and her followers an opportunity to harness primal forces that could tilt the balance of power in their favour. The Baroness's Werewolves were used for covert operations, their supernatural abilities making them perfect for missions that required stealth and brutality.

As the Baroness's power within the regime solidified, so too did the sense of dread that permeated the Berghof. Her demands grew more audacious, and she delved into areas of the occult that even Hitler had not dared to explore. The Baroness revelled in her dual existence, using her Werewolf abilities to enforce her will and eliminate those who opposed her.

Her influence was not without its challenges. Some within the Nazi Party viewed her and her followers with suspicion, fearing that their true allegiance lay with the Pack rather than with the Reich. Whispers of dissent emerged, but Hitler, blinded by his obsession with the occult, refused to heed them.

Hyde read on, learning more about the Baroness's treachery. According to Wilhelm Reinhardt's "Mystic Betrayal: The Hidden Saboteurs of Nazi Germany," the Baroness systematically undermined the Nazi regime. She fed Hitler and his inner circle selective information, steering them toward decisions that would destabilize their own plans. Her goal was to weaken the Nazi regime from within, creating chaos that she could exploit for her own gain. In doing so, she hoped to amass enough power to challenge the Pack's authority and establish herself as a dominant force in the supernatural world.

Elisabeth Schreiber's "The Dark Seductress: Unmasking the Baroness's Treachery" detailed how the Baroness manipulated relics and artefacts. Many of these items were genuine, imbued with ancient powers, but others were cleverly crafted fakes designed to mislead and ensnare. She wove intricate deceptions around these objects, convincing Hitler and his advisors that they held the keys to invincibility, all the while knowing they were traps that would eventually backfire.

Hyde had heard from Lisandra that the Baroness's ultimate betrayal came to light through a covert investigation initiated by a faction within the Pack. Alarmed by the increasing frequency of her transgressions, they dispatched one of their most trusted members to uncover the truth. This investigator, posing as an SS officer, infiltrated the Baroness's inner circle, carefully gathering evidence of her crimes and duplicity. The evidence was staggering. It proved that the Baroness was not only working against the interests of the Pack but also manipulating the Nazi regime for her own gain. The evidence was brought before the Pack's leaders, who were both horrified and enraged by her betrayal. However, the Baroness's power and influence within Germany made it impossible to move against her directly without risking exposure and greater conflict. As such, the evidence was buried, never having been permitted to be used against her.

The Pack's leaders became wary of her, monitoring her actions closely but biding their time. They knew that a direct confrontation would be too dangerous and could result in a devastating backlash. Instead, they waited, hoping that her own machinations would lead to her downfall. Luther had been able to verify much of this through various tomes in the museum from such writers as Professor Heinrich Müller, Dr Ingrid Bauer, and others.

The Baroness's plans were ultimately derailed not by the Pack but by the inexorable advance of the Allied forces. As the tide of war turned against the Nazis, her influence waned. The loss of the Nazi regime to the Allies brought about the collapse of the elaborate network she had built. Her carefully laid plans crumbled, and she was left isolated and powerless.

However, the Baroness's cunning and foresight ensured her survival. She had established numerous contingency plans and hidden resources that allowed her to maintain a degree of power and influence long after the fall of the Third Reich. She quietly transitioned her operations into the shadows, aligning herself with emerging power structures in the post-war world. Over the decades, she adapted and evolved, infiltrating new political and financial systems while continuing her pursuit of ultimate power.

The Pack, aware of her continued existence and wary of her capabilities, chose to monitor rather than confront her directly. Her ability to navigate and manipulate modern institutions, combined with her supernatural prowess, made her a formidable adversary. To this day, the Baroness remains a shadowy figure, her true intentions and ultimate goals a mystery, her legacy a testament to the enduring danger posed by those who seek power at any cost.

[Chapter 19] — The Gathering of Elders

Elders from every corner of the Underkingdom gathered in Grimlecht, their journeys long and arduous yet undertaken with unwavering resolve. From the snow-laden forests of Siberia to the arid stretches of the Australian Outback, the world's most revered werewolves made their way to the heart of the Pack's ancient city. Grimlecht's streets, usually cloaked in eerie silence, now bustled with a strange mix of urgency and solemnity as the Elder Council convened. This unprecedented assembly signified a pivotal moment, for the Council's decisions in these days would shape the fate of the Pack and all Werefolk for generations to come.

The air in the grand hall of Lord Tellus's estate was thick with tension as the Council of Elders convened. The room, adorned with ancient tapestries and relics of the Pack's storied past, felt oppressively heavy with the weight of history and tradition. Lord Tellus presided over the meeting, his piercing purple eyes observing the gathered Elders, each a leader in their own right.

Luther Hyde stood at the centre of the room, a figure of calm amidst the storm. His transformation from an ordinary schoolteacher to a powerful Werewolf, and now to the Alpha, had been nothing short of extraordinary. Yet, his status as a Turned Werewolf rather than a Pure Born made his position contentious. The Elders, a mix of both ancient and relatively younger Werewolves, murmured among themselves, casting sceptical glances at Hyde.

Hyde was wondering where Lady Lisandra was, she should be here to support him. Bembe was equally absent, and this raised a number of concerns for him.

"Order," Tellus commanded, his voice cutting through the low rumble of dissent. "We are here to discuss the recognition of Luther Hyde as the new Alpha. Let us proceed with decorum."

The first to speak was an Elder named Viktor, a grizzled Werewolf with centuries of experience from the Slavic Territories representing the largest portion of European Werewolves. "Lord Tellus, with all due respect, how can we place our trust in a Turned Alpha who was a schoolteacher just a few months ago? Our traditions have always favoured the Pure Born. How do we know he possesses the true strength of our lineage?"

Tellus nodded, acknowledging the concern. "Luther has proven himself through his actions and his strength. He has shown honour, wisdom, and the ability to lead. The circumstances of his transformation do not diminish his capabilities."

Another Elder, Lady Ingrid, added, "We have all seen the evidence of his deeds. He has defeated enemies that threatened our existence and brought unity to factions that were at odds. Is that not enough?"

Elder Roland Écuyer rose from his seat, his voice calm but resonant. "I stand in support of Luther Hyde as our Alpha," he began, his eyes sweeping across the council. "While some may question his origins as a Turned, it is undeniable that he has demonstrated the strength, integrity, and vision necessary to lead.

We must not let outdated traditions blind us to what is best for the Pack. Unity is our only path forward, and Hyde has proven his commitment to uniting not only the Argentum Lupus but all Werefolk. It is time to embrace a leader who represents both our past and our future."

Before anyone could respond, the Baroness stood up. Her presence was commanding, her crimson eyes holding a sinister gleam. "The evidence may show his physical prowess and cunning, but it does not change the fact that he is Turned. We cannot overlook our traditions so easily. The Pack's stability relies on adherence to our laws and customs."

Her words were met with murmurs of agreement from several Elders. The Baroness continued, her voice dripping with disdain, "We must ask ourselves if we are willing to risk our future on an anomaly. What guarantee do we have that he won't falter? That his Turned nature won't become a liability?"

Hyde stepped forward, his gaze unwavering. "I understand your concerns, Baroness. However, strength and leadership are not solely determined by one's birth. They are forged through experience, integrity, and the willingness to protect and guide our Pack. I may have been a schoolteacher a few months ago, but I have faced adversaries, both human and supernatural, and I have emerged victorious each time. I stand here not just because of my strength but because of my commitment to our Pack's future."

The Baroness's eyes narrowed, a cold smile curving her lips. "You speak well, Hyde, but words are easily spoken. Do you truly believe that loyalty can be earned so swiftly? You lack the centuries of tradition, the bloodlines that have defined our leadership since the beginning. You expect us to place our faith in someone who has known our world for mere months?" Her voice was laced with venom, though there was a flicker of unease behind her words.

Hyde met her gaze, his voice firm and resolute. "I do not expect trust to be given without question, nor do I seek to erase the legacies of those who came before me. But the Pack stands at a crossroads, one that requires not only strength but also the courage to adapt. The traditions that once protected us now threaten to divide us. It is time we remember what truly binds us: the desire for survival, honour, and a future free from fear and betrayal. My time among you may be short, but my commitment to these principles runs deep."

Hyde's words settled heavily in the air, a truth that seemed to echo through the chamber, challenging the old ways and the core of the Pack's future. The Elders exchanged tense glances, each of them grasping that the decision before them was more than just about leadership—it was a reckoning for the Pack itself. Would they continue to cling to ancient traditions, or was it time to accept change for the sake of their survival?

The Baroness stood defiant, her cold gaze sweeping the room. Yet, beneath her veneer of confidence, a flicker of something darker flashed in her eyes—an emotion she rarely showed: fear. Her influence, once thought to be untouchable, was now facing its greatest test before she could speak; however, Lord Tellus rose, his presence commanding the room.

"Enough," he declared, his voice steady but laced with a quiet intensity. "The time for rhetoric is over. What stands before us is not simply a question of who should lead but of who has betrayed us from within. Hyde's leadership is only one part of the conversation. We must now turn to the darker truth that has emerged—one that implicates the Baroness in a series of recent actions intended to weaken the foundation of our council itself."

The Elders leaned forward, their attention now wholly on Lord Tellus. "In recent months," he continued, his voice sharpening with each word, "there has been an undeniable pattern of deception, sabotage, and attempts to undermine my role as an Elder of the Pack. The theft of my leadership ring, the false accusations meant to discredit me, and the assassinations of key figures loyal to the council—all of these acts point directly to the Baroness."

The Baroness's face hardened, her defiance shifting to open disgust at the whole situation. "You have no proof," she spat.

But Tellus's gaze was unrelenting. "The evidence against you is overwhelming," he countered, his voice ringing with authority. "While we deliberate Hyde's worthiness as Alpha, we cannot overlook the crimes that have been laid bare before us—your treachery during the Nazi regime, your manipulation of sacred relics, and your betrayal of the Pack and the attempt to use the Third Reich to supplant the Council and name yourself sole leader. These offences demand justice, regardless of your bloodline or influence."

The chamber fell silent once more, every Elder's gaze fixed on the Baroness. Hyde's call for change had opened the path, but now the weight of the Baroness's misdeeds pulled the Pack closer to an inevitable reckoning. The moment of truth was at hand, and the chamber felt poised at the edge of history, the air thick with the anticipation of a long-overdue judgment.

The Baroness's eyes narrowed, a dangerous glint in them. "Those are accusations, Tellus. Old stories meant to undermine me. I have served the Pack in my way, and my methods, though unconventional, have always been for our benefit."

Hyde interjected, "Your actions have endangered us all. The Pack's unity is at risk because of your machinations. This cannot continue."

Before the Baroness could respond, Viktor rose, his voice cutting through the tense atmosphere with a note of urgency. "We must not forget the Baroness's lineage," he declared, his eyes sweeping over the gathered Elders. "She is the daughter of our previous Alpha, and by right of blood, she carries a claim to leadership that cannot be dismissed lightly. The traditions that have guided us for centuries hold bloodlines in the highest regard, and to overlook her heritage is to undermine the very foundation of the Pack."

He cast a challenging look at Hyde before continuing, "While I acknowledge the deepest laws of the Pack, which state that an Alpha's legitimacy does not depend solely on birth, we cannot simply cast aside the power of the bloodline that has ruled us for generations. The Baroness's claim is not born of ambition alone—it is rooted in the ancient traditions that have sustained us. To abandon these principles in favour of an unproven leader would set a dangerous precedent."

Lord Roland Écuyer rose, his commanding presence filling the chamber. His voice was clear and resonant as he addressed the council. "With respect to Elder Viktor's argument, we must remember that the core of our deepest laws is unequivocal," he began, his gaze fixed on Viktor. "The Alpha is not merely appointed, nor is the title passed down through bloodlines. It is a birthright of a different kind—an inherent destiny that cannot be manufactured or claimed by force."

He turned his attention to the assembled Elders, emphasizing his words. "Throughout our history, the Alpha has always been recognized not by lineage but by the very essence of their being. An Alpha is born as an Alpha; it is a matter of spirit, an undeniable presence that commands loyalty and trust from the moment it emerges. It is not a title to be inherited, but an innate calling that compels us to follow."

Écuyer's gaze settled on the Baroness. "While the Baroness may be the child of a former Alpha, birthright alone does not make her the Alpha we need. The Alpha is marked by destiny, and it is clear that the mantle does not rest on her. Luther Hyde, despite his origin as a Turned, has shown the undeniable traits of an Alpha—courage, integrity, and an unyielding commitment to the Pack's welfare. We must honour the laws that bind us, laws that acknowledge not just who was born to whom, but who was born to lead."

The Baroness's face contorted with barely contained fury. "My bloodline is pure, my right to lead unquestionably. How can we forsake our heritage for a Turned Werewolf?"

Tellus's voice was firm, "The laws are clear. The Alpha is determined by their ability to lead, not by their birthright. Luther Hyde has demonstrated his worthiness through actions, not just lineage."

The tension in the room was palpable. The Baroness's supporters glared at Hyde while others nodded in agreement with Tellus. The debate was fierce, with arguments flying back and forth. Hyde stood his ground, meeting each challenge with calm resolve.

As the debate raged on, a commotion erupted outside the hall. The doors burst open, and a young Werewolf, breathless and wide-eyed, ran in. "Lady Lisandra has been taken! We found signs of a struggle but no trace of her captors."

Chaos ensued as the Elders reacted with shock and anger. Hyde's heart pounded as he turned to Tellus. "We need to find her. Now."

Tellus nodded, his expression grim. "This council is adjourned. We will resume once Lady Lisandra is found and safely returned."

As the Elders began to disperse, Hyde noticed the Baroness slipping away towards a side exit. He moved quickly to intercept her, but she was already gone by the time he reached the door. The scent of cherry blossoms lingered in the air, a distracting lure that pulled at Hyde's senses—using the knowledge of Hyde's attraction for Lexie, the Baroness uses the momentary lapse in focus to slip away.

Hyde's mind raced. The Baroness had made her move, and Lisandra's kidnapping was a clear sign of her desperation and ruthlessness. He knew that finding Lisandra and exposing the Baroness's treachery was now more crucial than ever.

He turned to the remaining Elders, his voice firm and resolute. "We must act swiftly. Gather all available resources and search for Lisandra. And we cannot let the Baroness escape justice."

As the Elders mobilized, Hyde felt a surge of determination. The stakes were higher than ever, but he was ready. He would rescue Lisandra, confront the Baroness, and prove once and for all that he was the Alpha the Pack needed.

[Chapter 20] — The Hunt for Lady Lisandra

The moon hung low in the sky, casting an eerie glow over the ancient forest surrounding the Capital. The Council of Elders had just adjourned, and Luther Hyde, accompanied by a select group of trusted allies, plunged into the oppressive darkness. The trees whispered secrets of ages past, their gnarled branches reaching out like skeletal fingers as if trying to ensnare the intruders.

Lisandra's disappearance was more than a personal loss; it was a dagger aimed at the heart of the Pack's unity. Hyde knew that finding her was paramount, and he felt the weight of that responsibility like a shroud around his shoulders.

The search party moved cautiously through the dense underbrush, their senses heightened, alert for any sign of Lady Lisandra. The air was thick with the damp scent of earth and pine, but then a faint, familiar fragrance cut through—Lisandra's scent, a mix of wild lavender and something distinctly lupine. One of the scouts, a lean, sharp-eyed Werewolf named Kieran, lifted his nose to the wind and caught it first. "Over here!" he called out, his voice low but urgent.

The others quickly gathered, their focus sharpening as they followed the faint trace. The scent grew stronger as they pressed on, leading them deeper into the forest. Their hearts pounded with hope and anticipation, knowing that they were finally closing in on her location. It wasn't long before the dense foliage opened into a small clearing, the moonlight casting eerie shadows across the forest floor. The scent of Lady Lisandra was unmistakable now, lingering heavily in the cool night air.

But before they could react, figures emerged from the darkness—werewolves, fangs bared, with hostility in their eyes. Their leader, a hulking brute named Gregor, stepped forward, his eyes glinting with malevolent amusement in the dim light.

"Looking for someone, Hyde?" Gregor taunted his voice, a gravelly growl that sent shivers down Hyde's spine. "You should turn back. This forest isn't safe for traitors and their followers."

Hyde's eyes narrowed, his heart pounding in his chest. "Where is Lady Lisandra? Tell me now, and I might let you walk away."

Gregor's laugh was a sinister echo through the clearing. "Do you think you scare me, schoolteacher? You're nothing but a Turned Pup. You don't have the blood to lead us."

Hyde's response was swift and lethal. He lunged at Gregor, making the Change in the blink of an eye and shocking the challenger. The clearing erupted into chaos as Hyde's allies engaged the other loyalists. Claws slashed, and teeth gnashed, the air thick with the scent of blood and fur.

Hyde's strength and agility were unmatched. He moved with a predatory grace, dodging Gregor's wild swings and landing precise, bone-crunching blows. Gregor landed a few ineffectual hits on the young Alpha, but every hit from Hyde caused massive damage and sprayed Gregor's viscera upon the walls. Within moments, Gregor was on the ground, his eyes wide with shock as Hyde's claws pressed against his throat.

"Last chance. Where is she?"

Gregor coughed, blood trickling from his mouth. "You'll never find her… the Baroness… will end you…"

With a swift motion, Hyde bent and bit hard and deep into Gregor's throat, causing the latter's lifeblood to pour into the dirt and a wet, gurgling death rattle to emerge from what was left of the hulking Werewolf's neck. He stood, panting, his eyes scanning the battlefield. His allies had subdued the remaining loyalists. Hyde's voice was steady as he addressed his team. "Search them. We need any information they might have."

One of his allies, a Werewolf named Lena, found a crumpled note in one of Gregor's men's pockets. She handed it to Hyde, who quickly scanned the contents. "It speaks of an abandoned monastery deep in the forest," he read aloud. "Does anyone know of it?" Again, Lena stepped forward nodding and with a brief pointing in the direction they needed, they were off.

The group pressed on, guided by the cryptic directions on the note and Lena's knowledge of the area. The journey was arduous, the forest becoming denser and more foreboding with each step. Shadows danced menacingly, and strange noises echoed through the trees, creating an atmosphere thick with dread.

As the moon was reaching the horizon, they arrived at the ruins of the monastery, its once-majestic structure now a silhouette against the moonlit sky. The crumbling stone walls seemed to close in around them, the air filled with a palpable sense of foreboding.

Inside, they encountered another obstacle: an Elder named Cornelius, a staunch supporter of the Baroness. He stood at the entrance, his expression a mix of arrogance and disdain, his eyes glowing with an unnatural light.

"Hyde," Cornelius sneered, his voice dripping with contempt. "I should have known you'd come. But you're too late. That traitorous bitch is beyond your reach."

Hyde stepped forward, his voice cold and unyielding. "Move aside, Cornelius. This doesn't have to end in bloodshed." Even while speaking the words, he knew they were untrue.

Cornelius laughed, a hollow sound that echoed through the ruins, amplifying the eerie silence. "You don't have the resolve to kill an Elder, Hyde. You're weak. I have lived more than a thousand of your years, if you truly believe yourself capable of ending me, you are a bigger fool than any of us believe."

Hyde's eyes hardened, a chill running down his spine. "You underestimate me."

As the two came together in a clash of fur, claws and teeth, minions of the Elder spilt out to engage with Hyde's group. A young wolf, whom Hyde had not had the opportunity to even learn his name yet, succumbed to the ambush before he could even transform. His face was ripped away in jagged chunks by the claw of a brown-coloured villain.

The battle was fierce, the darkened ruins adding to the macabre atmosphere. Cornelius fought with a primal ferocity, his experience evident in every calculated move. But Hyde's determination and newfound power were quickly overwhelming the prowess of the millennia aged Elder. Again, the Elder slashed with all of his formidable strength, cutting furrows across the ribs of Hyde, but far shallower than he intended and, ultimately, needed. Luther turned into a beast from the nightmares of old with each searing tear in his skin. With a final, decisive blow, he incapacitated Cornelius, pinning him to the cold, damp ground.

"Where is she?" Hyde demanded, his voice a menacing growl.

Cornelius coughed, struggling to breathe, broken ribs deep cuts all over his body, causing rivers of crimson to splash on the ground beneath him, and yet his eyes filled with defiance. "You'll never… get to her… alive…"

Hyde tightened his grip, his face a mask of controlled rage. "Where?"

The Elder's eyes twirled with unfettered fear in his realisation that this was no meek and mild 'pup' as the Baroness had assured him but a ferocious and cunning wolf of legend. Cornelius's defiance wavered, and in a feeble attempt to save his life, his voice a strained whisper. "The catacombs… below… guarded…"

Hyde felt a pang of regret as he ended Cornelius's life, but he knew it was necessary. With a great swing of his arm, he decapitated the older wolf with one sweep of his claw. The head rolled across the ground, stopping at the feet of one of his surviving wolves and staring unblinking up at him. The Elder's remaining wolves kneeled in submission. Turning to his allies, he said, "We need to move. Quickly. Guard these wolves until the Council can determine what is to be done with them. Gather our wounded and dead and see they are ready to be moved when I return."

Hyde descended into the catacombs, the air growing colder and more oppressive. The walls seemed to close in around him, the darkness becoming almost tangible. Torches flickered along the damp stone corridors, casting long, wavering shadows that seemed to twist and writhe like spectral entities.

As he ventured deeper, he encountered a solitary figure – a Werelynx, alert and poised to strike. The Werelynx's eyes gleamed with murderous intent as he sprang at Hyde, claws extended.

Hyde dodged the initial attack, feeling the rush of air as the Werelynx's claws sliced through the space where his head had been moments before. The Werelynx was fast, almost too fast to track. Hyde spun around, using the Werelynx's momentum against him, and landed a solid kick to his side, sending him sprawling against the wall.

The Werelynx was on his feet in an instant, hissing and baring his fangs. "You should have stayed out of this, Hyde. Now you'll die down here with the rest of them."

Hyde didn't reply. He launched himself at the Werelynx, their bodies clashing in a violent dance of claws and fangs. The Werelynx was agile, slipping out of Hyde's grasp more than once, but Hyde's determination never wavered. He finally managed to catch the Werelynx's arm and pinned the killer to the wall behind him. Hyde ignored the repeated slashes coming from the smaller yet dangerous assassin's remaining claws and grabbed the throat of the Werelynx, showing the creature the full might of a being of much greater strength.

"Where is Lisandra?" Hyde demanded, his voice a growl of fury.

The Werelynx struggled, snarling. "I'll never tell you. You're already too late."

Hyde tightened his grip, his eyes blazing. "You will tell me. Or I will make you wish you had."

He reached for a torch from the nearby wall, pressing it against the Werelynx's skin. The scent of burning flesh filled the air as the Werelynx screamed in agony. "Talk," Hyde ordered, his voice a chilling whisper.

The Werelynx's screams echoed through the catacombs, the sound almost drowned out by the hiss of burning flesh. "Alright! Alright! She's in the chamber at the end of the tunnel… guarded by two of the Baroness's best…"

Hyde pulled the torch away, the Werelynx's screams fading into whimpers. "Thank you for your cooperation." He dropped the killer in a heap, leaving the Werelynx writhing in pain on the cold stone floor.

He reached the chamber, finding it empty except for the signs of a recent struggle. Lisandra had been here, but she was gone now. Hyde's heart sank as he saw the faint drag marks leading to a hidden passage. "They've taken her," he spat at the open air, his voice laced with frustration and fear.

As he moved through the hidden passage, the air grew colder and more oppressive. The walls seemed to close in around him, the darkness becoming almost suffocating. He emerged into another chamber, where the two guards the Werelynx had mentioned stood ready.

The guards, two hulking Werewolves with eyes that gleamed with malevolent intent, lunged at Hyde. The fight was brutal, the confined space making every move dangerous. Hyde fought with a ferocity born of desperation, his claws slashing through the air with deadly precision.

One of the guards managed to land a blow on Hyde, sending him crashing into the wall. Stars exploded in his vision, but he pushed through the pain, launching himself back into the fray. He tackled the guard, their bodies crashing to the ground in a tangle of limbs and snarls. With a final, decisive bite, Hyde ended the guard's life.

He turned to see the other guard recovering from a staggering headshot Hyde had given him only moments before. With a roar, Hyde charged, slamming into the guard and knocking him off balance. Again, using his prodigious strength, he overpowered the second guard, literally crushing the blood and air out of him, leaving him lifeless on the cold stone floor.

Hyde's heart pounded as he searched the chamber. In a corner, hidden behind a pile of rubble, he found Bembe, bound and unconscious but alive. He rushed to his side, cutting his bonds with trembling hands. "Are you alright?" he asked, his voice softening as he looked into his friend's eyes.

Bembe nodded weakly, though his eyes were filled with fear. "They have my mother," he whispered.

Hyde helped him to his feet, "I know. I was led to believe she was here. Have you seen her?"

"Yes, she was pulled out of here about ten minutes ago, but I did not see which way they went."

"We will find her; you have my word on that."

As they made their way back to the surface, Hyde's resolve hardened. The Baroness's treachery had reached its end.

[Chapter 21] — Rabid

The remaining members of Hyde's party arrived, guided by the sounds of fighting between Luther and the savaged loyalists.

Hyde turned to his companions, his voice urgent. "We need to divide our efforts. Lena, take Bembe and the prisoners back to the Elders. Ensure they're safe and get any medical attention they need. The rest of you, with me. We're going to find Lisandra."

Lena nodded, helping Bembe to his feet. "Be careful, Luther. We'll be waiting for your return."

Hyde watched as Lena and the others disappeared into the darkness, leading the wounded and prisoners back to the safety of the Elders. Breathing deeply through his nose, he caught the scent of Lady Lisandra. He turned to the remaining members of his team, his expression grim. "Let's move. We don't have much time."

They pressed on, the darkness closing in around them like a suffocating shroud. The air grew colder, and the sounds of their footsteps echoed through the narrow passageways. Every creak and groan of the ancient structure seemed to taunt them as if the catacombs themselves were alive, conspiring against their quest.

As they advanced, the sense of being watched grew stronger. Hyde's senses were on high alert, his heart pounding in his chest. They reached a fork in the path, and Hyde paused, his instincts guiding him. "This way," he said, leading them down the left corridor.

The cavern was pitch black, save for the faint glimmer of phosphorescent fungi clinging to the damp stone walls. Hyde and his companions moved cautiously; senses sharpened to the slightest sound or movement. The air was thick and foul, heavy with a musky stench that clung to their nostrils. Hyde led the way, every muscle tense, the oppressive darkness pressing in from all sides.

"Something's watching us," Rhea whispered, her breath barely audible, her eyes darting around the cavern's shadowed recesses.

Hyde nodded silently. He sensed it, too—an ominous presence lingering just beyond the edges of their perception. It was close, hiding in the darkness, waiting for its moment to strike. The only sound was the eerie drip of water echoing through the twisting tunnels beneath the monastery's catacombs.

Suddenly, a low, guttural growl vibrated through the cavern, a sound so primal it sent chills down their spines. Hyde's party froze, their Werewolf instincts flaring.

Without warning, a massive shape hurtled from the darkness, colliding with Hyde with brutal force. The two figures tumbled across the cavern floor, a tangle of fur, claws, and teeth. The creature's eyes burned with a strange, frenzied light, its movements erratic and unpredictable.

"Get back!" Hyde shouted, managing to kick the beast off him, sending it sprawling across the cavern. It landed on all fours, snarling viciously, its massive frame barely visible in the dim light.

Rhea and Kieran shifted to either side as they flanked the beast, trying to corner it. The creature was enormous, its muscles corded with unnatural strength, but its eyes betrayed an absence of reason— a mind lost to sheer madness.

The Rabid lunged at Kieran with terrifying speed, its jaws snapping inches from his throat. Kieran managed to dodge the attack, raking his claws across its side. The Rabid barely seemed to notice the wound, its focus entirely consumed by rage.

"It's not like the others," Rhea growled as she tried to get behind it. The beast twisted and lashed out, striking Rhea with a backhanded blow that sent her crashing against the cavern wall.

Hyde charged, his massive Werewolf form colliding with the Rabid in a burst of raw strength. The creature fought with wild abandon, its claws tearing into Hyde's flesh, but he didn't relent. He grappled with it, muscles straining as he tried to pin it down.

"It's a Rabid!" Kieran shouted, his voice filled with urgency as he circled around to help. "A Werewolf infected with Bloodmoon Fever—it's lost its mind completely! Pure rage, no control!"

The Rabid's response was a guttural roar, its fangs snapping at Hyde's neck as it struggled to break free. Hyde felt the searing pain of its claws raking his side, but he tightened his grip, using his superior size and strength to hold it down.

Rhea, recovering from the blow, lunged forward and sank her fangs into the Rabid's shoulder, trying to weaken its movements. The beast thrashed violently, managing to throw her off, but it was growing slower, its movements more erratic.

Kieran darted in, raking his claws across the creature's throat. The Rabid howled in agony, its blood spraying across the cavern floor. But it wasn't enough—it kept fighting, its body driven by a primal urge to kill.

Hyde summoned every ounce of his strength, his claws digging deep into the Rabid's chest. With a powerful twist, he aimed for its heart. There was a sickening crunch as his claws pierced through bone and muscle, finally finding their mark.

The Rabid let out a final, blood-chilling howl before collapsing, its body convulsing one last time before going still. Hyde's breathing was ragged, his fur matted with blood, both his own and the Rabid's. He stood over the fallen beast, a mix of relief and exhaustion settling over him.

Rhea and Kieran slowly approached, their eyes wide with a mix of awe and horror.

"That was… one of the worst I've seen," Rhea panted, her voice strained.

Hyde stretched his abused muscles, then wiped blood from his mouth. "The Baroness's madness runs deeper than we thought," he said, his voice low. "If she's using Rabids as weapons, she's more desperate than we realized."

Kieran shook his head. "Rabids are pure destruction. It takes dark magic to create one—someone who wants chaos and death more than anything else. The Baroness is playing a dangerous game."

The three of them stood in the darkness of the cavern, the echo of the Rabid's final howl still lingering. They had won this battle, but it was clear that the war against the Baroness's corruption was far from over. After a few minutes of searching the ring of the cavern walls, they found a tunnel in the far side of the cavern and began running through it. Before long, they came across a long-forgotten chapel.

As they approached the chapel, the faint sound of chanting reached their ears. The air grew heavier, the oppressive atmosphere almost suffocating. Hyde signalled for silence, his heart pounding in his chest as they crept closer.

They reached the entrance to the chapel, the heavy wooden doors slightly ajar. Hyde peered inside, his eyes adjusting to the dim light. The scene before him sent a chill down his spine.

The chapel was a macabre sight, its once-sacred walls now defiled by dark rituals. Candles flickered on the altar, casting eerie shadows on the grotesque symbols etched into the stone. In the centre of the room, surrounded by a circle of chanting loyalists, was Lisandra, bound and unconscious on the cold floor.

Hyde's blood ran cold. He knew they had to act fast. "We need to take them by surprise," he whispered to his team. "On my signal, we move in. Be prepared for anything."

The loyalists were deeply engrossed in their ritual, their chanting growing louder and more frenzied. Hyde's heart pounded in his chest as he gave the signal, and they burst into the chapel with a fierce determination.

The loyalists reacted with shock and fury, their chants turning into snarls and growls. The fight that ensued was chaotic and brutal. Hyde moved with lethal precision, his claws slashing through the air, cutting down anyone who stood in his way. His team fought with equal ferocity, their movements a blur of claws and fangs.

Hyde's focus was unyielding. He fought his way through the throng of loyalists, his eyes never leaving Lisandra. As he reached the centre of the room, a towering Werewolf lunged at him, its eyes filled with murderous intent. Hyde met the attack head-on, their bodies colliding with a force that shook the chapel.

The Werewolf was strong, its claws raking across Hyde's chest. Pain flared through him, but he pushed through it, his determination unyielding. He dodged a second strike and countered with a powerful blow to the Werewolf's side, sending it crashing to the ground. Before it could recover, Hyde delivered a final, decisive strike, ending the fight. A quick glance around the room for another opponent showed only that Rhea and Kieran had ended the remaining loyalists.

Breathing heavily, Hyde knelt beside Lisandra, cutting her bonds with hands that shook violently from adrenalin and fear. "Lisandra," he whispered, his voice filled with relief. "We're here. You're safe now."

Lisandra stirred, her eyes fluttering open. "Luther… you found me…"

Hyde helped her to her feet, his heart swelling with a mix of relief and determination. "We need to get out of here. The Baroness will pay for this."

Before they could take a step, Lisandra hissed in pain and dropped, Hyde's grip on her the only thing stopping her from slamming into the ground. She was clutching at her side.

Hyde was checking the side that ailed her and found a long-jagged tear in her skin, not of which caused him the most concern, but the blackened colour and putrid stench emanating from it did.

Lisandra confirmed the infection by telling him that this was how Werewolves get rabies through magical means, which is what the group of loyalists had been doing to her in the chapel.

Kieran walked up. "You just saw the results of the dark magic. It works similarly to regular rabies in that it strips the reason from its host, causing them to turn into angry, feral creatures. They are attempting to turn Lady Lisandra into a Rabid!"

"Is it similar to common rabies? As in, it takes days before the symptoms manifest?"

"Yes, but it's already too late. This is not a disease that can be simply treated at the hospital. The only ones who have managed to cure it are…"

The tension of the whole night and finding out the chase may have been for nought caused Luther to snap a bit more than he intended, "Are who dammit!"

It was the tired voice of Lisandra that answered, "The Ursa…"

The words hung as daggers in the ears of the party, for they all knew, even Hyde, that the Ursa were not known to have even a slight shred of sympathy for the Argentum.

Nevertheless, Hyde set his jaw and picked up the poisoned Elder, "It isn't over yet. I will speak with the leadership of the Ursa and either convince them to help or rip the knowledge from their corpses."

As they made their way back to the surface, the oppressive atmosphere of the catacombs seemed to close in around them. The darkness was suffocating, the shadows twisting and writhing as if alive.

The sun was beginning to rise over the dense forest as Hyde, Kieran, and Rhea emerged from the dark catacombs, their bodies battered and their spirits heavy. Lady Lisandra lay unconscious in Hyde's arms, her skin burning with fever. Despite her weakened state, she was alive—a small but crucial victory in their relentless struggle.

The group moved silently through the trees, each step taken with an urgency driven by Lisandra's condition. The reality of her plight hung over them like a dark cloud. The Rabid they had faced deep beneath the monastery was more than just a monstrous adversary; it was a harrowing reminder of what could become of one infected with Bloodmoon Fever. The same fate could befall Lisandra if they didn't act quickly.

Hyde's mind churned with conflicting emotions. Relief at having found Lisandra clashed with the grim understanding of what lay ahead. She was not just a fellow Elder; she was a friend, someone he had trusted and fought beside for as long as he had been part of the Pack. Now, she was reduced to a fragile figure in his arms, and the fever that raged through her veins felt like a betrayal of everything he had sworn to protect.

As they moved closer to Grimlecht, the reality of what needed to be done pressed harder on Hyde's conscience. The only known cure for Bloodmoon Fever lay in the hands of the Ursa. They are fierce enemies of the Pack—behemoths of the wilds, known for their strength, stubbornness, and mistrust of outsiders.

They arrived back at Grimlecht's gates, the towering walls providing a familiar but somewhat hollow sense of safety. Kieran and Rhea exchanged glances, each burdened with their own thoughts about the battle beneath the monastery and what it meant for their future.

Kieran's voice broke the silence as they approached the main gate. "What do we do now, Hyde?"

Hyde's gaze was distant, fixed on the horizon beyond the city. "We must go to the Ursa," he said finally, the weight of the decision clear in his tone. "They alone hold the key to curing Lisandra. There's no other way."

Rhea's face was etched with worry. "But the Ursa—what if they refuse? What if they use this as leverage against us?"

Hyde's eyes flashed with determination. "Then I will do whatever it takes to convince them. We cannot let Lisandra suffer for our past sins nor for the politics of old grudges. I swore to protect my Pack, and I intend to keep that promise."

But even as he spoke, doubt gnawed at him. Could he truly bridge the chasm between the Pack and the Ursa? Was it possible to heal wounds so deep, wounds that had been carved not just by swords and claws but by betrayal, fear, and centuries of hatred?

As they made their way through the city streets, Hyde tightened his grip on Lisandra, feeling the feverish heat radiating from her body. He couldn't let her die—not like this. The Baroness had brought enough darkness to their world; it would not claim another innocent life if he could help it.

[Chapter 22] — The Healer

The tension in the air of the Great Hall of Lord Tellus's estate was palpable. Luther Hyde paced back and forth, his mind racing. Lady Lisandra, one of the most influential Elders and a trusted ally, lay unconscious in a fevered state in the infirmary, her condition worsening by the hour. The magical rabies that had stricken her was unlike anything Hyde had encountered before. The Pack's healers were at a loss, their remedies proving ineffective against the affliction.

Hyde turned to the assembled Elders, his voice edged with desperation. "We need a cure. We need it now. I know the cure lies with the Ursa, but surely there is one among them I can speak to for help?"

Lord Tellus stepped forward. His eyes, filled with apprehension but deep understanding, met Hyde's. "The only race to have mastered the Bloodmoon Fever are the Ursa, and they are our sworn enemies. However, there is one who might be able to help. There is a healer amongst their number who puts the lives of her charges above the squabbling of our two Underkingdoms. Anya Volkov, she is a Kamchatka Werebear from Siberia. She's known for her extensive knowledge of ancient healing arts and her ability to combat mystical illnesses just as much as she is known for combat prowess. While I understand the necessity, and I do believe she will help, exercise extreme caution. She will likely believe you are an enemy first and foremost. But if anyone can save Lisandra, it's her."

Hyde's heart skipped a beat. "Where can I find her?"

Tellus handed Hyde an old, worn map. "Anya resides in the remote forests of Siberia. It won't be an easy journey, but we will reach her. We must. We will assemble a team immediately."

"I will go alone. If there is any hope of convincing Anya we are not a threat, it will be on my own."

Lord Tellus blanched. "Luther, I know you have strength that surpasses even the Werewolves with centuries, millennia of strength, but a Werebear is more than a match for even you."

"It is worth the risk."

Hyde gathered his essentials and set out in a loaded 4x4 Landrover on the frenzied trip to Siberia. Even with the rugged truck, the journey was gruelling, filled with treacherous landscapes and harsh weather. Hyde travelled alone, knowing that speed and appearing as little of a threat as possible were crucial. The thought of Lisandra's life hanging in the balance spurred him on, pushing him to his limits.

After a day of relentless travel, Hyde reached the edge of the dense Siberian Forest. The map showed that he would have to venture into the forest itself, and the way was far too overgrown for the truck, so Hyde drove it into a secluded space in a thicket of trees and parked it. He stepped out into the foreboding wilderness. The air was bitterly cold, the snow crunching under his boots as he made his way deeper into the dark, thick forest. He followed the directions on the map meticulously, his senses on high alert for any signs of danger.

As he ventured further, the forest seemed to close in around him, the trees towering like ancient sentinels. The silence was deafening, broken only by the occasional rustle of leaves and the distant howl of wolves. Hyde's mind raced with thoughts of Anya Volkov, hoping she would be willing to help him.

Finally, Hyde reached a clearing. In the centre stood a modest wooden cabin, smoke curling from the chimney. He approached cautiously, his heart pounding in his chest. Taking a deep breath, he knocked on the door.

No sooner had his hand struck the gnarled wood the second time when a massive weight slammed into the side of his head, sending the young leader flying through the air to slam into a tree on the far side of the clearing. The pain erupted from what seemed every cell of his existence as he struggled to right himself and face his attacker. He heard rather than saw what was coming to kill him at an alarming speed, not only for its sheer size but even for a member of the supernatural.

As a wolf, Hyde towered over his people at a staggering height of 8 feet. But the monster coming for him now was easily another 6 feet taller than him! Time appeared to slow as his vision finally cleared. He began to change. Something happened when he changed this time, however…

Luther had grown accustomed to the change of height he was as a human into the much taller Werewolf, but this time he had grown… even taller. He noticed other startling details as well, such as his arms and legs being significantly thicker and longer than they had been only a day before. He was momentarily distracted by his new, impressive and imposing physique. Fortunately for him, so was his quarry.

Once again, being in the presence of another member of the Werefolk, Luther's body took on the trait of the Werebear before him. Accepting the strength of a Werebear and the added height and bulk it provided him, Hyde quickly became one of the most powerful creatures in the history of Werefolk.

Confusion and wariness caused the enormous Werebear to slide to a halt a dozen paces from the intruder. She was still a good two feet taller than this wolf that had come into her territory, but wolves were not known to come anywhere near her height to begin with. She had intended on squashing this interloper immediately, but his change was so drastic that she decided to take a different tactic and spoke.

"What are you doing here, wolf?" Her bestial form caused her voice to take on a blood-chillingly low, threatening tone that any lesser being would likely have died from fright.

"Anya Volkov?" Hyde asked, his voice steady despite the urgency he felt.

"Yes," she replied, her voice was calm and steady, but caution tinged her Russian accent. "And you are?"

"I'm Luther Hyde, Alpha of the Argentum Lupus. I've travelled a long way to find you. I know our great houses have been enemies, likely even before either of us was born into this world, but we need your help. One of our Elders, Lady Lisandra, has been struck by a Bloodmoon Fever. Our healers can't cure it, but we've heard that you might be able to."

Anya studied Hyde for a moment, her eyes narrowing slightly. "What makes you think I wish to help save a member of our greatest enemy?"

"It is my understanding that you hold life before any feud, even one so old and bloody as ours."

"This may be true, but this does not answer the question, nor does it spur me to want to help those who have hunted my kind nearly to extinction in the past."

"You make valid points. I can only counter them with promises of action. Words are, in themselves, useless. But I have only recently come to the Argentum, and I am still trying to solidify my position as leader, but it is my deepest desire to mend the rifts between all of the Underkingdoms. I do not wish for this feud to continue, to possibly swallow one or more of our great houses into the void. I give you my word as the Alpha that I will do everything within my power to make genuine peace with the Ursa. Possibly starting with you…"

"There has never been an Alpha wishing to speak with us, much less bring peace. The former Alpha and his wretched offspring nearly obliterated my kind. Why should I believe you are any different?"

"Again, all I can offer is my word. However, I have not tried to return the blow I received in welcome at your door."

At that remark, the Werebear let a small chuckle escape her lips. "I must admit, you took it well."

"Anya, our two races will never have peace until there are those willing to trust enough to try."

Anya studied this Werewolf intently. Hyde could tell she was torn between wanting to try for the peace she clearly longed for and simply ripping him in two just to be certain.

"Wait here for one moment," she said not unkindly but still added, "Please."

She walked back to her cabin and went inside. A few short moments later she came to her door and stepped out, a tall, powerfully built woman with broad shoulders and a muscular frame instead of the menacing Werebear of a few moments ago. Her dark hair fell in wild waves to her mid-back, and her piercing icy blue eyes locked onto Hyde with a mix of curiosity and caution. She waved for him to join her. He transformed back, donned yet another fresh set of clothes she laid outside her door for him and made to enter the cabin.

Hyde followed her into the cabin, the warmth and cosiness of the interior a stark contrast to the icy wilderness outside. Anya motioned for him to sit by the fire, and he gratefully accepted, feeling the heat seep into his bones.

"Tell me more about how she got this disease," Anya said, sitting across from him and leaning forward attentively.

Hyde recounted everything he knew, describing the symptoms and the fruitless efforts of their healers. Anya listened intently, her expression thoughtful.

"So, it sounds as though the Baroness has finally stopped her quiet schemes and switched to full frontal assault," she said finally. "I can help your Elder; I even have all of the ingredients needed here. Before I will help, however, I need to know what you intend to do with that evil bitch."

Hyde was anticipating this, given her statement of "the previous Alpha and his wretched offspring".

"Oh, she will pay for all of her transgressions with her life," he said with complete finality.

Anya nodded at his words but had one question: "When?"

"The Elders and I already have search teams out looking for her. One team has already searched her estate in the Black Forest, but that château is empty. As soon as she is found, we will get her. Do you wish for yourself or another of your people to witness?"

She did not answer but smiled approvingly.

"I have the necessary herbs and knowledge to create an antidote," Anya replied. "But the process is delicate and requires time. We'll need to act quickly to save your Elder."

Hyde nodded, his determination unwavering. "Whatever it takes. I'm ready."

Anya stood, her presence commanding. "We'll start immediately. Follow me."

Hyde followed Anya to a back room filled with shelves of jars and ancient texts. The air was thick with the scent of herbs and incense. Anya began gathering ingredients, her movements swift and precise.

As she worked, Anya glanced at Hyde. "Why did you come alone, Alpha?"

"I did not want you believing that we were coming for a fight," Hyde replied. "I wanted to convey as little of a threat as I could. And I needed to ensure Lisandra's safety."

Anya nodded approvingly. "A wise decision. Now, let's save your Elder."

The hours that followed were intense, filled with the meticulous preparation of the antidote. Hyde assisted where he could, his focus entirely on the task at hand. Anya's calm and steady demeanour was reassuring, her expertise evident in every step she took.

Finally, the antidote was ready. Anya handed Hyde a small vial of the glowing liquid. "This should counteract the curse. Administer it to Lady Lisandra as soon as possible."

Hyde accepted the vial with a deep sense of gratitude. "Thank you, Anya. You've saved her life."

Anya's icy blue eyes softened. "It's my duty to help those in need. Go, Alpha. There's no time to waste."

With the antidote in hand, Hyde set off on the journey back to the Elders' estate. The forest seemed less foreboding now, the path clearer. He moved with renewed energy, driven by the hope of saving Lisandra.

As he travelled, Hyde couldn't shake the feeling that this was just the beginning. The alliance with Anya Volkov and the knowledge she possessed could be invaluable to the Pack. The road ahead would be challenging, but Hyde was ready to face it, united with allies old and new, in the fight to protect their world from the encroaching darkness.

[Chapter 23] — The Hunt for the Traitor

The grand hall of Lord Tellus's estate buzzed with nervous energy as Luther Hyde strode in, the vial of antidote clutched tightly in his hand. The journey back had been gruelling, but he had made it in record time, driven by the urgency of saving Lady Lisandra. The Elders turned to him, their eyes filled with a mix of hope and fear.

Hyde wasted no time, heading straight for the infirmary. Lady Lisandra lay on a bed, her breathing shallow, her skin pale and clammy. The sight of her in such a state filled Hyde with a renewed sense of determination. He uncorked the vial and carefully administered the glowing liquid to her.

For a moment, nothing happened. The room was deathly silent, everyone holding their breath. Then, a faint glow spread from Lisandra's chest, radiating outward. Her breathing steadied, and colour slowly returned to her cheeks. The Elders sighed in relief, murmuring prayers and thanks.

Hyde watched as Lisandra's eyes fluttered open, her gaze meeting his. "Luther..." she whispered, her voice weak but clear.

"You're going to be alright," Hyde said, his voice filled with relief. "Rest now. We'll take care of everything."

As the group made their way back into the Great Hall, he turned to the assembled Elders, his expression resolute. "We owe Anya Volkov our thanks. Without her help, Lisandra wouldn't have made it. We need to discuss forming an alliance with the Ursa."

The Elders exchanged wary glances, their expressions a mix of scepticism and curiosity. Lord Tellus stepped forward, his eyes thoughtful. "The Ursa have been our enemies for generations. Do you truly believe an alliance is possible?"

Hyde nodded firmly. "Yes, I do. Anya Volkov put aside our ancient feud to save Lisandra. If we can extend the same hand of friendship, we might find common ground. We need to put the past behind us and unite against the real threats we face. However, the Ursa will demand something from us in return."

Lord Tellus raised an eyebrow. "What is it they demand?"

"The death of the Baroness," Hyde said, his voice unwavering. "They see it as a means to remedy the blood feud between our nations. She has caused too much pain and suffering. Her death is a price we must pay for peace."

The Elders fell silent, the weight of Hyde's words sinking in. Lord Tellus finally nodded. "If that is what it takes to bring peace, then we must consider it. The Baroness has been a blight upon our people for too long."

The search for the Baroness continued with renewed vigour. Teams were dispatched to every corner of the Underkingdom, scouring the land for any sign of the elusive Werewolf. Hyde personally led several of these missions, determined to bring the Baroness to justice.

Days turned into weeks, the hunt relentless. The Baroness proved to be an expert in evasion, her tracks vanishing like smoke in the wind. Frustration grew, but Hyde refused to give up. He knew that capturing her was crucial to the Pack's future.

Hyde's every step echoed through the silent forest as he led his team deeper into the woods. The moonlight cast eerie shadows that twisted and writhed, creating phantom movements in the corner of his eyes. Every rustle of leaves and snap of twigs sent a shiver down his spine. The forest seemed alive with unseen threats, its silence a haunting prelude to the horrors they might uncover.

"We need to split up," Hyde whispered, his voice barely audible over the rustling leaves. "Cover more ground. Stay alert. She could be anywhere."

The team members nodded, their faces pale and tense. They dispersed into the shadows, each step taken with the dread of what might be lurking just out of sight. Hyde moved forward, his senses on high alert. The darkness pressed in around him, the cold seeping into his bones. The further he went, the more oppressive the atmosphere became.

Suddenly, a scream pierced the night, chilling Hyde to the core. He sprinted toward the sound, heart pounding. He found one of his men, Marcus, standing over a body—one of the Baroness's loyalists, eyes wide open in death, a look of pure terror frozen on his face.

"She's close," Marcus panted, his eyes wild with fear. "We have to find her before she finds us."

Hyde nodded, his resolve hardening. The Baroness's presence was a palpable threat, a dark force that seemed to suck the light and life out of the very air. They pressed on, every step a gamble with death.

Meanwhile, talks of unification with the Ursa progressed. Hyde and the Elders held several meetings, discussing the potential benefits and challenges of such an alliance. The debates were heated, old prejudices and fears surfacing, but Hyde's steadfast belief in unity began to sway even the most sceptical of the Elders.

One evening, as the Elders gathered in the grand hall, Hyde addressed them once more. "We have a chance to create something truly remarkable. An alliance with the Ursa could strengthen our defences, share knowledge, and bring an end to centuries of conflict. We must seize this opportunity."

Lord Tellus nodded, his expression thoughtful. "You speak wisely, Alpha. We will send an envoy to Anya Volkov and begin formal talks. But know that this will not be easy. Trust is hard to build and easily broken."

"I understand," Hyde replied. "But it's a risk we must take for the sake of our future."

As the Elders discussed the details of the envoy, Hyde's thoughts turned to the Baroness. She was still out there, plotting and scheming. But he was determined to bring her to justice, no matter the cost.

That night, as Hyde stood on the bridge overlooking the moonlit forest, he felt a sense of cautious optimism. The road ahead was fraught with challenges, but there was hope. With the support of allies like Anya Volkov and the possibility of uniting the Underkingdoms, they stood a chance against the darkness.

Hyde took a deep breath, the cool night air filling his lungs. The fight was far from over, but he was ready. With determination in his heart and a vision of unity in his mind, he prepared to lead his people into a new era—one of strength, unity, and hope.

The sudden sound of footsteps behind him made Hyde spin around, claws ready. A shadowy figure emerged from the darkness, the glint of moonlight revealing a familiar face.

"Anya?" Hyde breathed, lowering his guard slightly.

"Yes…" she replied. Her voice came ragged with pain, and he noticed her limp for the first time. "I received your message. I came to join in the peace talks and was attacked on the road by several Werewolves. Is this the peace you spoke of?!"

Despite her rage, he went to her and took her weight on one side. Even as she stared daggers through him and considered changing and killing him, he said, "You were attacked not by my order but at the word of our common enemy. I know it does not seem so, but you are safe here now. Are your attackers still of this world?"

"One or two may yet draw breath in the ditch where I left them."

"Will you allow our healers to tend to your wounds while I go out and find the cowards that attacked you?"

Anya thought long and hard about it. She wanted to trust this man if for no other reason than to save her people from another costly war, but to ignore a threat was the actions of a cub, something she was far from being, so she relented with a simple nod of her head.

The healers came at their Alpha's bidding quite quickly, but they hesitated at the sight of their patient. A stern look from Hyde was all that was needed to get them to move forward and help the large predator to their infirmary.

Without another word, Luther leapt from his perch on the bridge and into the night, even more blood splashing weighing heavily on his mind.

[Chapter 24] — Can He Trust Anyone?

The air was thick with tension as Luther Hyde sprinted through the dense forest, his senses attuned to the slightest sound. The moon cast an eerie glow over the landscape, illuminating his path but also casting ominous shadows that seemed to move with a life of their own. Hyde's mind raced as he considered the implications of the attack on Anya Volkov. Whoever had orchestrated this assault was clearly a threat to the fragile peace he was trying to build.

The forest was silent except for the sound of Hyde's rapid breathing and the crunch of leaves underfoot. He knew he was getting closer. The scent of blood and fear lingered in the air, guiding him toward the site of the ambush. Hyde's eyes narrowed as he spotted a clearing ahead, where the ground was disturbed, and the scent was strongest.

He slowed his pace, moving stealthily through the underbrush. As he approached the clearing, he saw the aftermath of the skirmish: bodies of Werewolves, some dead and others barely clinging to life. Hyde's eyes scanned the area, searching for any sign of movement. A faint groan caught his attention. He moved swiftly to the source, finding a severely wounded Werewolf, one of the attackers.

The loyalist's eyes widened in fear as Hyde loomed over him. "Please... don't kill me," he rasped, his voice weak from blood loss.

Hyde's expression was hard as he knelt beside the wounded Werewolf. "Who ordered the attack on Anya Volkov?"

The loyalist's gaze flickered with hesitation, but the pain was too much to bear. "Elder Viktor... he commanded us. Said we had to stop her from meeting you... said it was for the Baroness."

Rage boiled within Hyde, but he kept his voice steady. "Where is Viktor now?"

"He... he's at the old mill in the northern woods. Planning something... something big."

Hyde stood, his resolve hardening. He had to act quickly. He couldn't afford to let Viktor's plans come to fruition. He reached into his pocket and removed his phone, sending a brief text to Lord Tellus telling him what had happened and where the wounded were. He also instructed them to receive medical attention.

Hyde moved with purpose, his mind focused on the task ahead. The old mill was a relic from a bygone era, its decaying structure a stark contrast to the vibrant life of the forest. It was the perfect hideout for someone like Viktor, a place steeped in shadows and secrecy.

As Hyde approached the mill, he could sense the presence of others inside. The faint murmurs of conversation reached his ears, and he knew he had to act quickly. He transformed, his powerful Werewolf form blending with the darkness as he slipped through the broken windows and into the building.

Inside, the air was thick with tension. Hyde could see Viktor standing in the centre of the room, flanked by a group of loyalists. They were discussing their plans, oblivious to the danger lurking in the shadows.

Hyde's growl echoed through the room, drawing everyone's attention. Viktor's eyes widened in surprise, quickly followed by a sneer of contempt. "So, the Alpha has come to play," he spat.

Hyde's voice growled out of the inky black. "You've crossed the line, Viktor. Attacking Anya Volkov, endangering our chance for peace. You've betrayed the Pack."

As Hyde emerged into the dim light, his massive frame towering at twelve and a half feet tall, the room fell silent. His white fur gleamed eerily in the faint light, his presence commanding and terrifying.

Viktor's eyes widened in shock, quickly followed by a sneer of contempt that melted into fear. Fear of his own alpha drove him to say, "Betrayed the Pack? No, Hyde. I'm saving it. The Baroness is the true leader. You're nothing but a usurper."

With a snarl, Viktor signalled his loyalists to attack. The room erupted into chaos as Hyde clashed with Viktor's followers. He moved with deadly precision, his claws and teeth tearing through his opponents. Blood and fur flew as the battle raged on, the once-quiet mill now a cacophony of snarls and screams.

Hyde's focus was unwavering. He fought with a primal ferocity, his strength and speed unmatched. One by one, Viktor's loyalists fell, their defiance no match for Hyde's wrath. Finally, only Viktor remained, his eyes burning with hatred, though the fear was still evident.

"You will never be worthy, Hyde," Viktor hissed. "You'll never truly lead the Pack. The Baroness will return, and you'll fall."

Hyde lunged at Viktor, their bodies colliding with a bone-shattering force. They grappled, their claws raking across flesh as they fought for dominance. Viktor was strong, but Hyde's determination, righteous fury and new form gave him undeniable control over the outcome of this battle.

With a final, powerful surge, Hyde pinned Viktor to the ground. "It's over Viktor. You've lost."

Viktor struggled, his eyes wild with desperation. "You think killing me will change anything? The Baroness is still out there. She'll never stop."

Hyde's eyes flashed with an intense light. "Killing you? No, Viktor. I'm here to ensure you face justice."

Viktor laughed bitterly, his eyes filled with defiance. "You think you can scare me, Hyde? You're nothing but a pretender."

Hyde's new, formidable form loomed over Viktor, and as Luther slowly lifted the defeated Elder high into the air to face him, he finally realized the depth of his mistake. The sight of Hyde's twelve-and-a-half-foot tall, imposing frame with its pure white fur shattered Viktor's bravado. His mouth opened and closed as he struggled to find words.

"What are you?" Viktor stammered, fear gripping him.

"I am the Alpha," Hyde declared, his voice resonating with undeniable authority. "And you will face the consequences of your betrayal."

With a swift, incapacitating blow, Hyde rendered Viktor unconscious. Hyde stood, breathing heavily, his mind racing. The fight was over, but the war was far from won.

Hyde bound Viktor and the remaining loyalists, ensuring they couldn't escape. He sent a signal to his team, who quickly arrived to secure the area and prepare for the journey back to the Tellus's estate.

As they made their way through the forest, Hyde's thoughts turned to the future. The capture of Viktor was a significant victory, but it was only the beginning. The Baroness was still out there, and her threat loomed large. The Pack needed to unite now more than ever.

Back at the estate, Hyde presented Viktor to the Elders. The sight of the traitorous Elder in chains sent ripples of shock and anger through the council. Lord Tellus stepped forward, his eyes cold as he regarded Viktor.

"This betrayal cannot go unpunished," Tellus declared. "Elder Viktor will face the consequences of his actions. But we must also turn our focus to the Baroness. She is the root of this discord, and she must be stopped."

Hyde nodded, his resolve stronger than ever. "We will find her. And we will end this."

Meanwhile, talks of unification with the Ursa continued. The attack on Anya had shaken both sides, but Hyde's capture of Viktor and his commitment to justice began to rebuild trust.

[Chapter 25] — Earning Respect

The grand hall of Tellus's estate was filled with an oppressive silence as the Council of Elders gathered for the trial of Viktor. The ancient walls seemed to hum with the tension in the air, a testament to the gravity of the situation. Luther Hyde stood at the centre of the room, his presence commanding attention as he awaited the arrival of the accused.

Viktor was brought in, shackled and flanked by two of Hyde's most trusted warriors. His once-proud demeanour was now replaced with a look of defiance tinged with fear. The Elders watched with steely eyes as Viktor was led to the centre of the hall, his fate resting in their hands.

Lord Tellus, as the eldest and most revered of the Elders, took his place at the head of the council. His gaze was cold and unyielding as he addressed the room. "We are gathered here today to judge Elder Viktor for his acts of treason against the Pack. His betrayal and his attempt to sabotage our alliance with the Ursa cannot go unanswered. He has endangered us all by attacking Anya, the emissary of the Ursa, potentially throwing us into a bloody war the likes of which we have never seen nor likely to recover from."

A murmur of agreement rippled through the hall. Hyde could feel the weight of their collective judgment pressing down on Viktor, who stood with his head held high despite his chains.

"Elder Viktor," Tellus continued, "you are accused of conspiring with the Baroness to undermine the authority of the Alpha and to disrupt the peace we are trying to build with the Ursa. How do you plead?"

Viktor's voice was steady, though his eyes betrayed his inner turmoil. "I plead guilty, Lord Tellus. I did what I believed was necessary to protect the Pack from a false leader."

The Elders exchanged glances, their expressions hardening. Tellus nodded gravely. "Your guilt is clear, Viktor. Your actions have endangered us all. The penalty for treason is death."

Hyde stepped forward, his voice cutting through the tension. "I wish to speak on behalf of the accused."

The room fell silent, all eyes turning to Hyde. Even Viktor looked surprised, his defiance momentarily flickering into confusion.

"Viktor has betrayed us," Hyde said, his voice firm. "But I believe that, even with his age, he was misguided with loyalty and faith in one that is manipulative, and his death will only serve to deepen the divisions within our Pack. We need unity, not needless bloodshed. I have spoken with Anya, and while her rage is fierce and justifiable, she agrees that the one true villain in all of this is the Baroness. I ask that the Council show mercy and spare his life. Instead of death, I propose imprisonment for such a time as the Council feels he has repented his actions."

The Elders murmured among themselves, their expressions a mix of surprise and scepticism. Tellus raised a hand for silence. "Why should we spare him, Alpha? What reason do we have to believe he will not betray us again?"

Hyde met Tellus's gaze with unwavering resolve. "Because I believe that Viktor has a deep-set loyalty to the Pack, even deeper than anything he has for the Baroness, and I would not have that loyalty snuffed out for being misguided. He now owes his life to me, and while I know this will initially make him hate me even more, I believe time will show him that his true loyalty to the Pack is better served in helping me unite it once again. I believe that Viktor, despite his actions, still has a role to play. I cannot say what that role is as of yet, but it is something I believe in quite strongly."

Tellus considered Hyde's words carefully before turning to the council. "What say you, Elders? Shall we grant the Alpha's request?"

A tense silence followed, each Elder weighing the decision heavily. One by one, they nodded their agreement, though some did so reluctantly.

"Very well," Tellus declared. "Elder Viktor, you may not be willing to acknowledge it, but you owe your life to our Alpha. He clearly sees something in you that none of us does. You are hereby sentenced to imprisonment. You will remain in our custody until such time as the Council deems fit to release you."

Viktor's eyes flickered with a mix of relief and resentment. He turned to Hyde, his voice low and bitter. "Why...?"

Hyde met his gaze steadily, but he shocked him by saying, "I believe you are just as much a victim of the Baroness as anyone she has lashed out at in the physical world. I will admit that I am hoping that sparing your life will inspire you to want to help us take the

Baroness down once and for all, but only you can decide that. I stand by my decision regardless."

For a moment, Viktor remained silent, his eyes filled with a storm of emotions. Finally, he spoke, his voice laced with reluctant respect. "I do not wish to owe you my life. However, despite everything that has happened, I cannot deny an honourable action from any man. You do not have my loyalty, but... you have my respect. There are several places she might be hiding. The old monastery in the Carpathian Mountains, the abandoned castle in Transylvania, and the ancient ruins in the Black Forest. These are her most likely hideouts."

Hyde nodded, committing the locations to memory. "Thank you, Viktor. Your cooperation is appreciated."

As Viktor was led away, the Elders began to disperse, their expressions thoughtful. Hyde stood alone in the grand hall, his mind racing with the new information. The path ahead was fraught with danger, but he felt a renewed sense of purpose. The Baroness would be found, and justice would be served.

The moon hung high in the sky as Hyde and his team set out to search the locations Viktor had revealed. The journey was arduous, the terrain treacherous, but they pressed on with determination. Each site held its own dangers, but the possibility of capturing the Baroness drove them forward.

The first stop was the old monastery in the Carpathian Mountains. The air was thin and cold, the silence oppressive as they navigated the winding paths. The monastery loomed ahead, its ancient stones weathered by time. Hyde's senses were on high alert, every shadow a potential threat.

They searched the monastery thoroughly, but it was clear that the Baroness was not there. Hyde felt a mix of relief and frustration as they moved on to the next location: the abandoned castle in Transylvania.

The castle stood like a sentinel against the night sky, its turrets reaching towards the heavens. Hyde could feel the weight of history pressing down on them as they entered the crumbling halls. The air was thick with dust and the scent of decay, the silence broken only by the sound of their footsteps.

As they explored the castle, Hyde couldn't shake the feeling that they were being watched. As he searched, he finally spotted them: small security cameras stuck in various places throughout the castle. The shadows seemed to shift and dance, and he could hear faint whispers echoing through the corridors. But once again, the Baroness eluded them.

Their final destination was the ancient ruins in the Black Forest. The trees towered above them, their branches intertwining to create a canopy that blocked out the moonlight. The forest was alive with the sounds of nocturnal creatures, the air heavy with the scent of damp earth.

The ruins were a labyrinth of crumbling stone and overgrown vegetation. Hyde moved cautiously, his eyes scanning the darkness for any sign of movement. As they ventured deeper into the ruins, he felt a growing sense of dread.

Suddenly, a figure stepped out from the shadows, their presence almost ethereal in the moonlight.

"You've come a long way, Alpha," the woman said, her voice a soft, mocking whisper. "But you'll never catch her."

Hyde's eyes narrowed. "Who are you? What is your connection to the Baroness?"

The woman's smile was enigmatic, her eyes gleaming with a dangerous light. "All in good time, Alpha. All in good time."

Before Hyde could react, the woman vanished into the shadows, leaving him with more questions than answers. He clenched his fists, frustration boiling within him. The Baroness was still out there, and the hunt was far from over.

As the first light of dawn began to break through the trees, Hyde knew that their mission was far from complete. They would continue the search, relentless and unwavering. The Baroness would be found, and peace would be restored to the Pack.

With a deep breath, Hyde turned to his team, their faces reflecting the same determination that burned within him. They would not rest until the threat was eliminated and the future of their world was secured.

The hunt had only just begun.

[Chapter 26] — A Plan Begins to Form…

The cold light of dawn filtered through the dense canopy of the Black Forest, casting long shadows across the ruins. Luther Hyde stood in the clearing, his mind racing with thoughts of the Baroness and her elusive nature. The encounter with the mysterious woman had left him with more questions than answers, and the hunt for the Baroness was far from over. But for now, they needed to regroup and plan their next move.

Back at the estate, Hyde gathered Lisandra and Bembe in the grand library. The room was filled with ancient tomes and maps, their spines cracked and faded from centuries of use. The air was thick with the scent of old paper and dust, a stark contrast to the tension that hung in the air.

Lisandra was already poring over a map of the region; her brow furrowed in concentration. Bembe sat at a nearby table, flipping through an old book on the history of the Underkingdoms. Hyde joined them, the weight of the mission pressing heavily on his shoulders.

"We need to approach this strategically," Hyde said, his voice steady despite the turmoil within. "The Baroness is cunning and resourceful. We can't afford to make any mistakes."

Lisandra nodded, her eyes still fixed on the map. "Agreed. We need to narrow down her potential hideouts. The information Viktor provided is valuable, but we need more specifics."

Bembe looked up from his book, his expression thoughtful. "There are records here that mention various strongholds used by the Baroness's ancestors. If we cross-reference those with the locations Viktor mentioned, we might be able to find a pattern."

Hyde leaned over the table, studying the map with Lisandra. "Let's start with the Black Forest. The ancient ruins there are a known stronghold for the Baroness's lineage. If she has any connections to her past, she might seek refuge there."

Lisandra traced a finger along the map, marking the ruins' location. "We'll need to be thorough in our search. The Baroness has likely taken precautions to hide her presence."

Hyde nodded, his mind already working on a plan. "We'll split into smaller teams to cover more ground. Bembe, I want you to focus on gathering any additional information from the records. We need to know every possible location the Baroness could be hiding."

As Bembe nodded and returned to his research, Hyde turned his attention to Lisandra. "We also need to solidify our alliance with the Ursa. The execution of the Baroness will go a long way, but we need more than just a common enemy. We need trust and cooperation."

Lisandra looked thoughtful. "Anya Volkov is a key figure in the Ursa community. If we can gain her support and demonstrate our commitment to peace, it will help build a stronger alliance."

Hyde considered her words carefully. "We'll need to work closely with Anya. Show her that we are serious about this alliance and that we value her people. Actions speak louder than words, and we need to prove ourselves."

Bembe looked up again, his eyes gleaming with an idea. "What about the Manō hae? If we could form an alliance with them as well, it would strengthen our position even further. The Underkingdoms need unity now more than ever."

Hyde nodded, his mind racing with possibilities. The Manō hae, the mysterious shark folk of the seas, were known for their strength and prowess in battle. An alliance with them could be a game-changer.

"But how do we approach them?" Lisandra asked, her tone cautious. "The Manō hae are secretive, almost to the point of myth. They inhabit every sea on the planet, and their ways are unknown to us."

Hyde leaned back, his eyes distant as he thought. "A delegation could be sent after we have dealt with the Baroness and showed the Ursa we can be trusted. Showing them that we are serious about peace and unity is going to be difficult at best, but to approach them still as two separate nations will do us no favours. If we can present a united front with the Ursa, it might persuade the Manō hae to join us at the table for discussion, if nothing else."

Lisandra nodded slowly. "It's a risk, but it's worth taking. Long have our three people been driven apart by the power-hungry. It clearly does not work, as our races have been killing one another for centuries. The humans show even more examples of how division kills nations."

Bembe closed his book with a determined snap. "I'll start gathering information on the Manō hae. We need to understand their culture and what might appeal to them."

As the three of them continued their discussions, the atmosphere in the library grew more intense. They knew that the road ahead would be challenging, but they were determined to see it through. The Baroness was a formidable foe, but with the right allies and a well-thought-out plan, they stood a chance of bringing her to justice and uniting the Underkingdoms.

As the hours turned into the late evening, Hyde made a decision. "We need Anya with us in this," he said, his voice cutting through the quiet of the library. "It's not just about showing our trust, but also about pooling our resources. She has knowledge that could be invaluable."

Lisandra nodded in agreement. "Having Anya here would also demonstrate our commitment to the Ursa and to the alliance we hope to build."

Hyde rose from his seat. "I'll go to her personally. It's important that she understands how much we value her help."

Hyde left the estate and made his way to the guest quarters where Anya was staying. The night was cold, and the wind howled through the trees, creating an eerie atmosphere. He knocked on her door, and after a moment, it opened to reveal Anya, her expression one of curiosity and caution.

"Anya, may I come in?" Hyde asked, his tone respectful.

She nodded and stepped aside, allowing him to enter. The room was sparsely furnished but warm, a fire crackling in the hearth.

"What brings you here, Alpha?" Anya asked, her piercing blue eyes studying him intently.

He looked into her eyes with a look of inner turmoil. He knew that defined lines were necessary, but his entire life, up to this point anyway, had been getting everyone on equal ground around him. So, he made a choice: "You do not need to call me Alpha. You are neither my subject nor beneath me in any way. And I believe one of our best steps towards unity is by shedding any notions of unearned hierarchy."

Anya nodded thoughtfully, clearly processing his words before looking back and saying, "I appreciate your point of view, and I further appreciate that you are placing me on equal footing. However, I must point out that I am not the leader of my clan. I have been tasked with being the emissary, but I am not on the same level of leadership as you. I will stop calling you Alpha as per your request, but I must insist on treating you with deference to your position. If for no other reason than your current grasp of that position is still tenuous."

He absorbed her words thoroughly and was pleased to see a change in her view of him. He nodded graciously.

Hyde took a deep breath. "We're working on gathering information about the Baroness's potential hideouts and discussing ways to solidify our alliance with the Ursa. We also need to consider reaching out to the Manō hae. As our ally and the emissary to the Ursa, I would like you to join us. Your knowledge and perspective would be invaluable."

Anya's expression was of total incredulity. "You want me to join your council? To share in your plans?"

"Yes," Hyde replied. "It's important that we work together, not just as allies but as partners. I believe one way to accomplish this is in transparency and inclusion. We need to trust each other if we're going to succeed. And I wish for the Argentum and the Ursa to be spoken of as one."

Anya considered his words for a moment before nodding. "Very well… Luther. I will join you."

Hyde smiled, relieved. "Thank you, Anya. Your presence will make a difference."

Together, they returned to the grand library, where Lisandra and Bembe awaited them. Anya's arrival was met with respectful nods, and she took a seat at the table.

"Anya," Lisandra began, "we've been discussing our next steps. We need to solidify our alliance with the Ursa beyond the execution of the Baroness. What do you suggest?"

Anya leaned forward, her gaze thoughtful. "Trust is built through actions, not words. We need to show the Ursa that we are committed to their well-being. We have been solitary for centuries as joining together in groups proved to just draw in Argentum wrath." This statement brought on some shamed glances from Bembe and Lisandra. "Would you and your council be opposed to giving the Ursa land with which to unite into a city much like Grimlecht? In that spirit we could do joint ventures, shared resources, and mutual support in times of need. These are the things that will forge a lasting bond."

Hyde nodded. "I will have to take it up with the Council, but I will push for this because I believe it is a great means of showing we want this peace."

This news clearly pleased Anya as her shoulders relaxed, carrying unknown tension.

"Beyond this alliance, we need to consider the Manō hae. We know they are in Bermuda, as this is where I was Turned, and they clearly showed… displeasure at this."

Bembe interjected, "You mean when they tried to kill you in that cage?"

Lisandra just shook her head, but Anya looked understandingly.

Anya said, "They are fiercely independent and value their secrecy. I know they have the strictest rules of any of the Underkingdoms when it comes to turning someone. As we all know, most humans do not survive the bite of an immortal. And leaving bitten humans for the human authorities to find greatly threatens that secrecy. We will have to try and mend that particular slight before anything else. They inhabit every sea on the planet and have a deep connection to the oceans. They respect strength and honour but are wary of outsiders. I believe Luther can convince them, given his strength and abilities. Forming a lasting relationship with the Ursa will also go a long way toward bringing them to the table."

"We'll need to approach them carefully," Hyde said. "Show them that we are serious about peace and unity. If we can gain their trust, it would mean an era of peace so profound…"

As the group continued their discussions, the atmosphere in the library grew more intense. They knew that the road ahead would be challenging, but they were determined to see it through. The Baroness was a formidable foe, but with the right allies and a well-thought-out plan, they stood a chance of bringing her to justice and uniting the Underkingdoms.

Hours passed as they pored over maps, books, and records, piecing together the puzzle of the Baroness's movements and the best way to approach their potential allies. The room was filled with the soft rustle of pages turning and the quiet murmur of voices, a stark contrast to the storm brewing outside.

As night fell, Hyde looked up from his work, his eyes meeting Lisandra's. "We have a lot of work ahead of us, but I believe we can do this. We have to. For the sake of the Pack and the future of the Underkingdoms."

Lisandra nodded, her expression resolute.

With a renewed sense of purpose, Hyde, Lisandra, Bembe, and Anya continued their work, driven by the hope of a better future. The hunt for the Baroness was far from over, but they were ready for whatever challenges lay ahead. The storm was gathering, but together, they would face it head-on.

[Chapter 27] — Malice in the Shadows

The moon hung high in the sky, casting a silvery light over the dense canopy of the Black Forest. The estate, nestled within the ancient streets of the Capital, stood as a fortress of knowledge and power. Within its grand library, Luther Hyde, Lisandra, Bembe, and Anya continued their work, their discussions growing more intense as they delved into the mysteries surrounding the Baroness and the potential alliances they needed to forge.

Unbeknownst to them, a pair of eyes watched from the shadows, hidden deep within the blackness of the alley he stood in. The watcher remained silent, his presence undetectable to the keen senses of the Werefolk. He observed their every move, his gaze filled with disdain.

The watcher, known only by his self-given title, the Seer, had always held a deep contempt for what he called the "Grounders" — the Werefolk who roamed the earth. To him, they were nothing more than primitive creatures bound by their earthly limitations and petty squabbles. His true identity was shrouded in mystery, and even the oldest legends of the Underkingdoms spoke of him only in hushed whispers.

The Seer was no ordinary being. He possessed a deep and ancient knowledge, one that spanned millennia. His connection to the celestial realms granted him powers beyond the comprehension of mortal and immortal alike. He had seen the rise and fall of countless civilizations, and he knew that the Grounders were but a fleeting moment in the grand tapestry of time.

As he watched the Werefolk in the grand library, the Seer's thoughts turned to the approaching celestial event — the close passing of Halley's Comet, set to coincide with a total solar eclipse in a year's time. This rare alignment of celestial bodies held great significance for the Seer. He believed that it would herald the birth of a new group of Werefolk, ones who would transcend the limitations of their ancestors and rise to a new level of power and influence.

"The Grounders," he muttered to himself, his voice barely a whisper in the cold night air. "They are so consumed by their own conflicts and ambitions. They cannot see the larger picture, the grand design that the cosmos has in store for them."

The Seer's plan was intricate and far-reaching. He had spent centuries preparing for this moment, studying the movements of the stars and the cycles of the cosmos. He believed that the alignment of Halley's Comet and the solar eclipse would create a unique opportunity — a moment when the very fabric of reality would be altered, allowing for the emergence of a new breed of Werefolk.

But the Seer knew that this event would not go unnoticed by the Grounders. They would see it as a threat, an anomaly that needed to be controlled or destroyed. He needed to act swiftly and decisively, ensuring that his plans came to fruition without interference from the Werefolk.

As he watched Hyde, Lisandra, Bembe, and Anya, the Seer felt a twinge of irritation. Their alliance-building efforts were commendable but ultimately futile in the face of the cosmic forces at play. They were mere pawns in a much larger game, and the Seer was determined to be the one who controlled the board.

"The Grounders will never understand," he mused. "They are bound by their earthly concerns, unable to see beyond the horizon of their own existence. But I will show them. I will guide them to their true potential, whether they realize it or not."

With a final glance at the estate, the Seer melted back into the shadows, his presence disappearing as quickly as it had appeared. He had much to do in the coming year, and every moment counted. The Grounders would continue their search for the Baroness and their efforts to forge alliances, but they would soon learn that their true enemy was far greater than any single being.

The Seer would ensure that the alignment of Halley's Comet and the solar eclipse would bring about a new era for the Werefolk. Whether it would be an era of enlightenment or destruction remained to be seen, but one thing was certain — the Grounders would never be the same again.

[Chapter 28] — The Future...?

The search for the Baroness had reached an uneasy stalemate. Despite the relentless efforts of Luther Hyde and his party, the elusive Werewolf remained hidden, her whereabouts a mystery. The urgency of their mission had not diminished, but the leads had grown cold. Hyde knew that they needed to regroup and refocus their efforts. With the hunt temporarily slowed, it was time to turn their attention to the pressing matter of solidifying their alliance with the Ursa.

The grand hall of the estate was abuzz with activity as Hyde, Lisandra, Bembe, and Anya prepared for a crucial meeting with the Council of Elders. The air was thick with anticipation, and the weight of their collective hopes rested heavily on Hyde's shoulders.

The Council of Elders sat in a semicircle around the room. Their expressions were stern and contemplative as they awaited Hyde's proposal. Lord Tellus sat at the centre, his piercing eyes fixed on Hyde. Luther knew that while he technically had the leadership of the Pack, these men and women needed to be consulted to ensure cooperation. While cooperation was necessary, he was prepared to force this particular issue regardless of how they felt about it.

Hyde stepped forward, his voice steady and resolute. "Thank you for convening on such short notice. As you all know, our search for the Baroness has encountered some difficulties. While we continue to pursue every lead, we must also focus on building the alliances that will ensure our future stability and security."

The Elders nodded, their attention unwavering. Hyde took a deep breath and continued. "Anya Volkov has been invaluable in aiding us, and it's clear that the Ursa are willing to consider an alliance. However, we need to go beyond mere words. Also, the simple goal of eliminating a common enemy is a paltry point to hinge our alliance together. We must go beyond this step, crucial though it may be, and offer true peace by offering them territory long held by the Argentum. We must provide the Ursa with a territory they can call their own."

Immediately the chamber hummed with murmurs, some acknowledging the necessity, others outright condemning it.

A voice cut through the growing consensus, sharp and filled with scepticism. "And why should we trust the plans of a Turned?" Elder Mathias, a staunch traditionalist, stood with a look of disdain. "We are to place our future in the hands of someone who wasn't even born into our race? Who's to say he won't betray us, just as the Baroness did? Do any of you genuinely believe that he will not take this alliance with our oldest of rivals and supplant us all?"

The tension in the room spiked, and murmurs of agreement echoed from a few corners. Hyde felt a pang of frustration but maintained his composure.

"Mathias," Lord Tellus interjected his tone stern, "Hyde has proven himself through action, not just words. He has shown strength, leadership, and a commitment to our Pack's future. We cannot ignore the value he brings."

Mathias scoffed. "Strength? Perhaps. But loyalty? Leadership? I have not seen these actions. Yes, he helped rescue Lady Lisandra, and he captured the dissident Viktor. But his kind has always been fickle. The Turned do not have the same bond to our traditions, our laws."

Hyde stepped forward, his gaze locked on Mathias. "And to what laws and traditions do you speak of? The very laws that permitted the Baroness to continuously risk our Pack's safety? To pervert our existence and make our reputation be seen as little more than beasts? Or is it the traditions that have kept us isolated from the other Underkingdoms? Constantly getting members of our Pack killed in a feud that no one, not even Lord Tellus, can recall? I understand your reservations, Elder Mathias. But let me make this clear: my loyalty is to the Pack. To our survival and our future. I have no desire for division or betrayal. We are stronger and united, and that includes embracing those who are different. But it also means we must drop our prejudices and antiquated ways of doing things."

Another Elder, Helena, stood and added her voice. "Hyde's actions have shown his commitment. We must look beyond our prejudices if we are to forge a stronger future. The Ursa alliance is an opportunity we cannot afford to miss. You all know of the family and loved ones I have lost to the war with the Ursa, but even I cannot deny that this is the safest way forward."

Elder Mathias remained obstinate, "I will not support this *Alpha* until I am shown just cause to do so." His words were regrettably met with the nods of a few other traditionalists on the Council.

Lord Tellus stood again, gaining silence. "We can discuss this matter further once we have all of the information. Lisandra, you hold a map. Have you found a location where this possible city may be constructed?"

Lisandra stepped forward, unfurling a large map of the region on the table. "We've identified several potential locations for the Ursa's new territory. Each has its own advantages and challenges, but all are suitable for building a safe and thriving community."

The Elders leaned in, examining the map closely. Hyde pointed to a particularly promising location. "This area, a few hundred miles south of Grimlecht, is strategically located. It's close enough for mutual support but far enough to allow the Ursa their independence. The land is fertile, and there are natural resources that can be utilized for construction and sustenance. Additionally, it offers the same seclusion from humans that Grimlecht enjoys."

Outright rage emanated from another Elder, Olbricht. "You propose to move our sworn enemy practically to our gates?! Have you all forgotten the wolves we have lost to those monsters?"

Anger caused Anya to step forward but a steadying hand from Hyde stopped her.

"And do you not realise that there are many within their community that speak of us in the same manner? That *we* are the monsters in the dark moving to consume them? I know that both sides have their reasons to fear this alliance." Short barks of derision at the comment about fear. "Openly scoff the notion that you are afraid all you like, but I can see and smell the fear on you."

Again, Lord Tellus nodded thoughtfully and attempted to insert an optimistic air. "A promising location indeed. But what of the costs and logistics of building a new city?"

Bembe stepped forward, holding a detailed report. "We've consulted with the Ironclaw Guild, the foremost experts in construction and engineering. Their leader, Master Darius Ironclaw, has agreed to meet with us to discuss the project. He has provided us with an initial estimate of the costs, which include materials, labour, and infrastructure. The total cost is significant, but it is an investment in our future."

Hyde took over, his voice firm. "We propose that the costs be divided between our two nations. The Argentum will provide the initial funding and resources, while the Ursa will contribute manpower and additional resources as needed. This will ensure that both sides are equally invested in the success of the project."

Anger flushed on many faces at the prospect of having to front the initial cost, so Anya, attempting to soothe the verbal wounds, spoke up. "The Ursa are willing to contribute their strength and skills to this endeavour. We understand the importance of having a place to call our own, and we are prepared to work alongside the Argentum to make this vision a reality."

The room was divided, the tension palpable. Hyde knew he needed to bridge this gap. "If my being Turned is a point of contention, then let my actions continue to speak for me. We face threats that require unity and cooperation. The Baroness is still out there, and we need every ally we can get."

Lord Tellus nodded. "Well said, Hyde. We must move forward. However, perhaps we should shelve this discussion for now. Allow emotions to ebb, and cooler heads prevail. Please, everyone, let us settle the matter of the successor to Viktor. The Slavic region needs a leader, and they should have a vote on this matter regardless."

The discussion shifted; the atmosphere was still charged but focused. Names were proposed, debated, and finally, a decision was reached. Elder Ivan Petrov, a respected leader known for his strategic mind and fair judgment, was chosen to succeed Viktor.

With the new Elder in place and the plan for the Ursa territory not completely dead, Hyde felt a mix of accomplishment and frustration. The path ahead was fraught with challenges, but they were making progress.

Later that day, Hyde and his party made their way to the headquarters of the Ironclaw Guild. The guild hall was a massive structure, bustling with activity. Master Darius Ironclaw, a burly Werebadger with a commanding presence, greeted them warmly.

"Welcome, Alpha Hyde," Darius said, his voice a deep rumble. "I hear you have a grand project in mind."

Hyde nodded. "Indeed, Master Darius. We seek to build a new city for the Ursa, a place where they can thrive and live in peace. We need your expertise to make this vision a reality."

The Werebadger looked at him sceptically, "Has the Council agreed yet? I had heard they were not of one mind on this."

Hyde sighed, "They haven't yet. But I am remaining optimistic at the very least."

Darius nodded and led them to a large conference room, where detailed blueprints and charts were spread out across the table. "We've done a preliminary assessment of the proposed location. It's a good site with plenty of resources. However, there are challenges we need to address, such as the terrain and the infrastructure required to support a new city."

Bembe handed Darius the report. "We've outlined the costs and a proposed timeline for the project. We aim to have the city ready for habitation within a year, with construction starting as soon as possible. Not everything needs to be completed, but housing is the number one priority so the Ursa can continue to work where they live."

Darius studied the report, nodding thoughtfully. "This is a massive undertaking, but it's doable. We'll need to mobilize our workforce and secure additional resources. The timeline is tight, but with proper coordination, we can meet your goals."

Hyde looked at Anya, then back at Darius. "We're committed to making this happen. The Argentum will provide the initial funding and resources, and the Ursa will contribute manpower and additional resources as needed. We need to show the Ursa that we are serious about this alliance and that we value their partnership."

Darius smiled, his eyes gleaming with determination. "You have my support, Alpha Hyde. We'll begin preparations immediately. This will be a historic project, one that will shape the future of our people."

Anya spoke up, "I know this puts a damper on everything further, but the leadership of the Ursa will not make a move until you visit them yourself, Luther. I explained the complications with that, but they will not change their minds on it."

Bembe stiffened immediately, but Hyde cut off the cautious wolf, "I actually assumed this eventuality. I would not commit to moving my entire people without seeing who I am, trusting face to face and in a vulnerable position. I will go and speak with them. Alone."

Everyone there held their collective breaths. The alliance was of the utmost importance, but to allow their leader to go to a known hostile location solo was less than ideal to say the least. It was Darius who cut through the tension.

"I am sure that if an alliance is as important to them as it is to us, you should have no troubles." He meant to be reassuring, but even he did not look like he believed his own words.

As they left the Ironclaw Guild, Hyde felt a renewed sense of purpose. The path ahead was still fraught with challenges, but they were taking concrete steps towards building a better future for the Underkingdoms. The hunt for the Baroness would continue, but for now, their focus was on unity, trust, and cooperation.

Back at the estate, Hyde and his party gathered once more in the grand library. The discussions continued late into the night, their plans taking shape with each passing hour. They were determined to see their vision come to fruition, to create a world where the Argentum and the Ursa could live in harmony.

As the first light of dawn began to break, Hyde looked around the room at his companions. "We've made great progress, but there is still much to do. The Baroness is still out there, and we cannot rest until she is brought to justice. But for now, let us focus on building a foundation of trust and cooperation. Together, we can achieve anything."

With renewed determination, Hyde, Lisandra, Bembe, and Anya continued their work, driven by the hope of a better future. The storm was still brewing, but they were ready to face it head-on, united in their cause and unwavering in their resolve.

[Chapter 29] — Dagger in the Dark

The night once again had settled over Grimlecht, a heavy blanket of darkness that seemed to hold its breath. Luther Hyde found himself wandering the silent halls of the estate, his mind a whirlwind of thoughts. The alliance with the Ursa was progressing, but the weight of leadership, the stall in cooperation from the Council, and the ever-present threat of the Baroness kept his nerves taut.

In the dim light of the grand hall, Elder Mathias stood by a window, his silhouette sharp against the moonlit landscape. Hyde had exchanged tense words with him earlier, the friction between them palpable. Mathias, ever the traditionalist, had made no secret of his disdain for Hyde's position as Alpha, given his Turned status. Hyde sighed, pushing the thoughts aside. He needed rest.

Unbeknownst to him, shadows moved with intent elsewhere in the estate. A figure, sleek and silent, slipped through the corridors, its presence a ghostly whisper. The Werelynx from the Silentstrike Order had its orders—eliminate Elder Mathias and leave a trail that pointed to Hyde. The plan was to sow discord and suspicion, weakening Hyde's leadership from within.

Hours later, the tranquillity of the night shattered with a blood-curdling scream. Hyde jolted awake, his senses immediately on high alert. He rushed to the source of the sound, the great hall from whence he had been a mere hour prior, his heart pounding. The grand hall was filled with panicked Elders, their faces pale with shock. At the centre of the chaos lay Elder Mathias, his lifeless body sprawled on the floor, a pool of blood spreading around him.

Hyde's breath caught in his throat. He pushed through the crowd, kneeling beside Mathias. The Elder's throat was slashed, the wound precise and brutal. Hyde felt a cold dread settle in his gut. This was no ordinary murder.

Lord Tellus's voice cut through the din, commanding and stern. "Everyone, calm yourselves. We must handle this with care. Luther, you were seen in here while Mathias had been as well, what do you know of this?"

Hyde looked up, meeting Tellus's gaze with a mix of anger and confusion. "I know nothing of this, Lord Tellus. I was in my quarters until I heard the scream. It is true, I had seen Elder Mathias standing by that window," he said, pointing, "but we never exchanged words before I left to retire for the night."

A murmur of doubt rippled through the crowd. Hyde felt their suspicion like a physical blow. Whispers of "he hated Hyde" and "Hyde was frustrated" danced around the room, boiling Luther's blood with every syllable.

Again, Elder Helena stepped forward. However, her expression was grim but placatory said, "We must investigate thoroughly before making any accusations."

The Council dispersed, the Elders returning to their quarters with heavy hearts and troubled minds. Hyde remained, his thoughts racing. He knew the Baroness was behind this, but proving it would be another matter entirely.

In the following days, the investigation unfolded, led by a team of Elders and trusted guards. They scoured the estate for clues, their scrutiny intense. Hyde assisted where he could, his frustration mounting as they found nothing to exonerate him. The tension among the Council was palpable, the seeds of distrust already taking root.

Then, amidst the chaos, a single piece of evidence emerged—a small, intricately carved bead found near the scene of the crime in a crack between the marble floor panels. At first glance, it seemed insignificant, but given the extensive cleaning of the estate daily, it was suspicious. The bead's presence was a subtle but telling sign.

The bead was brought before the Council by the guard who had found it. Many were ready to write it off as a simply discarded bauble, likely from one of their own persons, but others knew that the cleaning was meticulous and knew it belonged to whoever killed the Elder.

An unnamed Elder from the South Pacific region stepped forward and said, "Lord Tellus, this bead is from the Silentstrike Order. I recognise it from dealings I have had with their Order. I can't say who it belongs to specifically, but taking it to their leader would yield results. She does not tolerate sloppiness and likely will tell us who ordered this murder as recompense for their failing."

Tellus examined the bead, his expression thoughtful. "This is a delicate matter. The Silentstrike Order operates in shadows. We are stronger than they are, but that does not mean we can control them. I know where one can meet the leader, but who will meet with the dagger in the dark?"

Immediately, Hyde spoke up. "I will, of course. This may be a perilous task, but we need answers. They hoped to wrap this around my neck and sow discord amongst us. I will go to the Silentstrike Order and seek out this Werelynx."

Many were against the idea of Hyde going to ascertain his own innocence, but with Tellus's reluctant approval, Hyde set out on his journey with Lena, a member of Lord Tellus's territory. The Silentstrike Order's headquarters was a closely guarded secret, known only to a few. None of which resided amongst the Council, so Tellus told them of the meeting place in Berlin. A pub known as The Velvet Claw.

They left immediately, driving straight from Grimlecht to Berlin, arriving a few short hours later. As they approached the tavern, a few Werelynx standing outside eyed them warily as they approached, their sleek forms tense and ready for action but otherwise appearing like any normal passersby's. They stepped inside, indifferent to their audience.

Hyde walked up to the bar and whispered the passphrase Lord Tellus had told him; the bartender nodded and disappeared through a set of doors behind the bar. Minutes later, a woman walked up to Hyde and led them into a dimly lit chamber, where the leader of the Silentstrike Order awaited—a formidable Werelynx with eyes that gleamed like polished onyx.

"State your business, Alpha," the leader intoned, her voice a silky threat.

Hyde held up the bead. "One of your assassins killed the Elder Mathias and left this behind. I was meant to be the one held responsible, so I want the name of the operative who handled the job."

The leader's eyes narrowed. "And precisely, why should I give you their name? We are not in the habit of selling out our people."

Hyde took a step forward. "To spare yourself and your organisation future embarrassment of one who leaves evidence to their crimes."

The leader studied him for a long moment before nodding. "We do not leave traces; this is true. I can tell you who was responsible. But it will come at a bit of a price…"

"What do you need?"

"When you find him, kill him. Upon hearing of him leaving this piece behind, which has led Werewolves to our doors, has earned him an execution. But I will tell you who he is if you will handle this for me."

Reluctantly, Hyde simply nodded.

"Very well. The one you seek is named Kael. He is loyal, but he has been making far too many mistakes. He boards himself in an abandoned factory at the edge of town. Find him, and you may find your answers, and I will be rid of a mess."

With this new lead, Hyde felt a glimmer of hope. He would find Kael, uncover the truth, and clear his name. The path ahead was perilous, but he was ready to face it head-on.

[Chapter 30] — Means to an End

The shadows lengthened as Luther Hyde and Lena, Lord Tellus's ward, approached the abandoned steel factory on the outskirts of Berlin. The dilapidated structure loomed ominously against the darkening sky. Hyde's senses were on high alert, every sound amplified in the eerie silence. Lena moved beside him with quiet confidence, her sharp eyes scanning their surroundings.

Hyde had been pleased Lena had been chosen to accompany him not just for her keen instincts, but also because of her unique connection to the Council. She was trusted by Lord Tellus and had proven her loyalty time and again. As such, he was favoured by the Council for this task. As they neared the entrance, Hyde signalled for silence. They slipped inside, their footsteps echoing softly in the vast, empty space.

The factory was a maze of rusting machinery and crumbling concrete. The air was thick with the scent of decay and neglect. Hyde led the way, following the faintest traces of Kael's scent. The Werelynx was a master of stealth, but even he could not completely erase his trail from Hyde's keen senses.

As they ventured deeper into the factory, the tension grew palpable. Hyde could feel Lena's steady presence beside him, a reassuring reminder of their purpose. They reached a dimly lit corridor, the walls lined with old lockers and broken tools. Hyde's eyes narrowed as he spotted a faint outline of a boot print in the dust and grime of the floor. Apparently, this fellow was pretty sloppy.

"This way," Hyde whispered, motioning for Lena to follow.

They moved cautiously, their senses attuned to the slightest hint of movement. The corridor opened into a large chamber, its ceiling high and shadowed. At the far end, they saw a figure standing beside an old furnace—Kael, the Werelynx assassin.

Kael's eyes widened in surprise as he saw Hyde and Lena approach. "How... How did you find me?" he demanded, his voice a low growl. "I left no trace. At any rate, we were never supposed to—" As he spoke, Lena shifted into her wolf form, using the spoken confrontation as the distraction she needed to change.

Hyde cut him off by stepping forward, his expression grim. "You underestimated us, Kael. You left something behind at the scene of the crime." He held up the bead before tossing it to the killer, who caught it easily.

Kael's eyes flicked to the bead, then back to Hyde. His confusion was evident, but it quickly turned to defiance. "I did not leave this behind…" His eyes narrowed, recognising what this "visit" was now.

Before Hyde could respond, Kael lunged at him, his claws extended. Hyde met him head-on, their bodies colliding with a force that reverberated through the chamber. Hyde matched the strength of the changed Werelynx despite not changing himself, his supernatural strength bleeding through to his human form.

Lena circled around, her eyes locked on Kael. She moved with a fluid grace, waiting for an opening. Hyde's strength and determination matched Kael's agility and ferocity, their struggle a deadly dance.

In a final, desperate move, Kael broke away from Hyde and charged at Lena. She sidestepped with a swift motion, bringing her claws in a precise arc. Kael staggered, blood seeping from a deep wound in his side.

Lena seized the opportunity, closing the distance and pinning Kael to the ground. "Who hired you, Kael?" she demanded, her voice a low growl. "Tell us, and maybe we'll show mercy."

Kael's eyes flickered with pain and defiance. He spat blood, a twisted smile on his lips. "You think... you know the truth? It was..."

Lena's eyes widened in shock; a knife had seemingly sprouted from the wounded creature's throat. Thus ended the life of Kael, the Werelynx assassin.

Lena turned on Hyde, prepared to tear into him for stopping the man from speaking the truth, when she saw the blade in his now limp hand. He had clearly been poised to run her through, but Hyde had saved her life.

Lena was troubled as she stood. Clearly, Kael intended to say something prior to his death but couldn't. She wanted to end this suspicion of Luther but did not know how now. It was then that Hyde, having searched Kael's bag, found a note from the Baroness ordering him to kill one of the Elders. It did not say to frame Hyde, but then again, it did not really need to.

Together, they left the abandoned factory, the weight of their mission pressing heavily upon them. The evidence was there but far more circumstantial than Lena had been hoping for, though Luther seemed relieved.

As they made their way back to the estate, Hyde's mind raced with the responsibility of his actions. He had eliminated a major block to his goals of uniting the Argentum with the Ursa, but it has cost the lives of two individuals. Reluctantly, he just pushed the thought from his mind, excusing it as an end with justified means…

[Chapter 31] — The Weight of Decisions

The shadows of the city deepened as Luther and Lena made their way back to the estate. A heavy fog settled over everything. The failure to fully ascertain the truth made physical by the gloom hanging over the world. The weight of their mission pressed heavily upon them, but for Hyde, an even greater burden lay hidden within his mind. As they navigated through the narrow streets, the events at the abandoned steel factory replayed Hyde's thoughts with haunting clarity.

Kael's lifeless eyes, the blood-stained floor, and the twisted smile of the assassin were etched into Hyde's memory. He had acted to save Lena, to prevent Kael from delivering a fatal blow, but he also stopped the assassin from revealing that it had been Hyde who ordered the murder of Elder Mathias, and the implications of his actions gnawed at his conscience. Hyde had always considered himself one who upheld justice and righteousness. But now, with two lives taken in the pursuit of his goals, he found himself teetering on the edge of a moral precipice.

Lena sat in the passenger seat beside him, silent and focused, her mind likely occupied with the implications of their encounter. Hyde could sense her trust in him, her belief that they were on the right path. But he couldn't shake the feeling that he had crossed a line from which there was no return.

As they reached the estate, Hyde excused himself from Lena, needing a moment alone. He walked through the grand hall, the flickering candlelight casting eerie shadows on the walls. Each step echoed with the weight of his internal struggle. He made his way to a secluded room, shutting the door behind him and leaning against it with a heavy sigh.

The room was dimly lit, filled with old books and artefacts that spoke of the Pack's history. Hyde moved to a large, ornate mirror, his reflection staring back at him. The face that looked at him was familiar, yet it felt foreign. The eyes that once held unwavering conviction now carried a shadow of doubt.

Hyde clenched his fists, his thoughts a turbulent storm. He had justified Kael's death as a necessary act, a means to protect Lena and ensure the secret was intact. But deep down, he knew that no matter the cost, they must unite with the other Underkingdoms. He loathed the manipulative nature, but he also understood that a leader must sometimes do the dastardly to protect the righteous.

What bothered him the most was the way he had broken the block to his peace accord. Mathias had been the main blockade into the solidification of the alliance with Ursa, but having him killed, effective though it may have been, was… lazy. Convincing those of opposing views may be difficult in the extreme, but there was more honour in pushing an argument than slipping a knife between ribs in the darkness.

The note from the Baroness ordering Kael to kill one of the Elders was a stroke of luck as he had nothing more he could have used to convince the Council of her treachery. But shifting through Kael's pack had afforded him the way to give the Council their evidence, bind them to a single goal, and protect his own machinations in the shadows.

"Am I becoming like her?" Hyde whispered to his reflection, his voice barely audible. The question hung in the air, a chilling reminder of the path he was on. With a sudden burst of rage and self-disgust, he slammed his fist through the antique mirror, shattering it and his reflection into a million pieces and cutting his hand to shreds.

He held up his ruined hand and watched with a detached air as the skin slowly knitted itself back together, his thoughts churning over the similarities of his actions to the Baroness, the puppet master behind so much suffering. She was a symbol of everything he fought against—deceit, cruelty, and a thirst for power. Yet, in his pursuit of justice, he had mirrored her actions in a way that felt irreparably wrong.

Hyde sank into a chair, his head in his hands. The image of Mathias, murdered to frame him, flashed in his mind. He had been so focused on the peace he was trying to create with this alliance that he had lost sight of the principles he once held dear. The line between right and wrong had blurred, leaving him in a moral grey area that felt suffocating.

His thoughts drifted to the Council of Elders, the trust they had placed in him, and the vision of unity he had fought so hard to achieve. Could he continue to lead them if he couldn't even trust himself? The weight of his decisions bore down on him, threatening to crush the resolve he had always prided himself on.

Hyde took a deep breath, trying to steady his racing thoughts. He had to find a way to reconcile his actions with his principles. He couldn't allow himself to become a monster in the pursuit of justice. The Pack needed a leader they could believe in, one who stood for more than just survival.

As the night wore on, Hyde wrestled with his inner demons. The darkness outside perfectly exemplified the turmoil within him. He knew he couldn't undo what had been done, but he could strive to be better. To find a way to achieve his goals without sacrificing his soul in the process.

Rising from the chair, Hyde faced his reflection once more. "I will not become her," he vowed, his voice stronger this time. "I will find a way to lead with honour and integrity, no matter the cost."

He resolved there and then that while he would not shirk from the distastefulness of killing to protect the Pack and the alliance, he would strive to stay on the righteous path and not dishonour himself again.

[Chapter 32] — Taking the Step Forward

The grand hall of the estate was once again filled with the tension of expectation as Luther Hyde and his party stood before the Council of Elders. The recent events weighed heavily on everyone's minds, but Hyde was determined to secure the future of the Pack and their alliance with the Ursa. This time, he had to win over the entire Council, including those who were previously reluctant.

Lord Tellus called the meeting to order, his gaze sweeping across the room. "We gather today to finalise our plans for the new territory for the Ursa and to ensure the support of all Elders in this crucial endeavour. Luther, you have the floor."

Hyde stepped forward, his voice steady and resolute. "Thank you, Lord Tellus. Elders, we have reached a pivotal moment in our quest for unity and stability. The Ursa have shown their willingness to work with us, and it is imperative that we demonstrate our commitment through action. The proposed territory offers the seclusion and resources needed for the Ursa to thrive. Today, I seek your support to break ground on this new site and move forward with our alliance."

Elder Mathias's replacement, Elder Ivan Petrov, spoke up first. His reputation for strategic thinking made his opinion highly respected. "The location you've chosen is indeed promising, Hyde. However, the logistics and costs involved are substantial. How do you propose we manage these challenges?"

Bembe stepped forward, holding the detailed report he had from the last meeting. "We've consulted extensively with the accountants of the Pack. If we pool our resources, and divide things equally, each faction will need to commit 250 million euros each. We know this is an incredibly substantial number, but given our longevity, each faction has more than enough to cover this and recoup it in a short amount of time."

A murmur of approval rippled through the Council, but Hyde could sense the lingering reluctance in some of the Elders. He took a deep breath and continued, "I understand that there are concerns, especially about the potential risks and the commitment required. But I assure you, this alliance is not just about the immediate benefits. It's about securing a future where our people can live in peace and cooperation. I urge you all not to focus solely on the money as a loss but as an investment in our future. The Ursa do not share our financial resources, but they are ready to stand with us, and we must show them that we are equally committed."

Elder Mathias's former allied faction, led by Elder Elias, voiced their scepticism. "Hyde, you ask us to trust a Turned leader and to invest heavily in a project that might not yield immediate results. What guarantees do we have that this alliance will truly benefit us?"

Hyde met Elias's gaze, his resolve unwavering. "There are no guarantees in life, Elder Elias. But there is one certainty: without unity, we face a future of continued conflict and division. Analysts from our various factions all agree that if we do not do something drastic, we could fall forever. Now Turned or not, the trust needs to be in the shared vision of unity. The Ursa has already shown us a great deal of trust by sending Anya here, deep amongst their enemies. And they further showed trust in us, allowing *us* to find the villain responsible for attacking that very emissary! Asking for trust in two such monumental situations was no less than asking them for the world. And they gave it. Now, when asked to show trust, not even at the same level, do we dare, *dare* deny it to them? I know each of you are people of deep honour and respect and would give your lives for your factions. Do not disappoint now when all that is required is your assent. Together, we are stronger. Divided, we are vulnerable."

Lena boldly stepped forward, her voice calm but firm. "I have seen firsthand the efforts and sacrifices Hyde has made for the Pack. He has proven his loyalty and his commitment. We must look beyond our prejudices and embrace the opportunity for a stronger future."

Elder Elias's eyes flashed with disapproval as he addressed Lena. "Mind your words, girl. You may be close to Lord Tellus, but you are not an Elder, and you would do well to remember your place here."

As Lena hung her head, cowed by the rebuke, Lady Ingrid interjected, her voice measured but resolute. "It is true; Lena is not an Elder, and she is aware of that fact. Yet, her words carry the weight of truth, nonetheless. It is precisely the perspective of those like her, who see our Pack's struggles up close that we cannot afford to dismiss."

The room fell silent, the weight of her words sinking in. Lord Tellus stood, his presence commanding. "It is time to decide. Those in favour of moving forward with the new territory and solidifying our alliance with the Ursa, raise your hands."

One by one, hands rose around the room. The reluctant Elders hesitated but eventually joined the majority. The decision was unanimous.

Lord Tellus nodded approvingly. "The Council has spoken. We will break ground on the new site and move forward with our plans. Hyde, you have our support."

A sense of relief washed over Hyde as he stepped back, his mission accomplished. But he knew that this was just the beginning. The real work was about to start.

Later that day, Hyde, Lisandra, Bembe, and Anya travelled to the proposed site, a lush expanse of land surrounded by dense forest. The air was filled with the scent of pine and earth, and the sounds of nature created a serene backdrop. They stood together, envisioning the future city that would rise from this ground.

Master Darius Ironclaw and his team from the Ironclaw Guild were already present, ready to begin the initial assessments. Darius approached Hyde, a determined glint in his eye. "We're ready to start, Alpha Hyde. This is going to be a project for the history books."

Hyde nodded. "Thank you, Master Darius. Your expertise and dedication are invaluable. Let's begin."

As the first shovels broke the ground, Hyde felt a renewed sense of purpose. This was the start of a new chapter for the Argentum and the Ursa, a step towards a united future.

With the groundbreaking ceremony complete, Hyde knew it was time to solidify the alliance with the Ursa. Anya approached him, but he was already nodding.

"I know it is time. Let us get the first four walls raised, and we can leave."

Anya understood and assisted, shortening the time by hours thanks to her own prodigious strength.

As they were preparing to leave, however, a box truck pulled into the clearing that no one knew. Darius was waving at it, attempting to get the driver's attention, when Luther noticed there was no driver.

No sooner did Hyde yell in alarm did the truck explode. The explosion was not excessively big, but what flew from the fireball wreaked so much damage that you would have thought a bomb from the Great War had dropped amongst them.

Darius had disappeared in the blaze, and Anya and Hyde were flung through the air like blades of grass in a strong wind. Metal fragments from the truck and screws and nails flew in every direction, ripping devastating holes in any being unfortunate enough to be in the radius.

Hyde sat up, his vision blurred liked he was underwater. He tried to stand, but extreme dizziness made him fall against a nearby tree. He shook his head, trying to clear it, when he noticed that despite seeing many screaming and crying, he could not hear anything. He reached up and touched his ear, felt a sticky wetness and looked at his fingers. Eardrums were completely wiped out from the concussive force. He closed his eyes and attempted to will himself to stop feeling so dizzy.

Anya appeared at his side, holding his arm to help steady him. He quickly looked her over and saw only a gash on her forehead. "ARE YOU OKAY?" he managed.

"Mmm… mmm…" was all he could get.

"I THINK MY EARDRUMS WERE RUPTURED."

She nodded and pointed to herself before giving him a thumbs up.

"HOW BAD IS IT?"

Her face darkened immediately.

Bad…

Epilogue

The cold, biting wind cut through him as he crouched motionless, watching the mountain villa on the slope across from him. Despite the frigid air that would have sent any normal man running to the warmth of a hearth, he remained focused on his goal. He knew his target was inside; he had seen her arrival an hour earlier. Patience was crucial now—rushing this would jeopardise the mission and allow their foe to once again slip from their grasp.

As he waited for the meeting to conclude, his mind wandered. He never asked to be a leader and never sought to make decisions that determined the future, or lack thereof, for others. Yet, here he was, ordering the elimination of those who opposed his leadership. These decisions gnawed at him like a dog with an old bone, filling him with fear that he was becoming the tyrant he dreaded.

After two and a half hours, the meeting broke. He watched dispassionately as, one by one, her supporters left, their cars gliding noiselessly through the falling snow. Soon, only she and her security team remained. He waited another hour to ensure no one would return before he gave the signal—a simple sound resembling the cough of a stag, a warning call hunters know well.

The signal marked the start of the settling phase of the plan. They would allow the occupants and security team time to settle into their night-time routines, ideally becoming complacent as boredom set in.

In the silence of the night, the slow, hypnotic snowfall drew his mind into deep reflection. The road to hell has always been paved with good intentions, and though his goals for the Pack were noble, the pervasive thoughts of becoming an undying dictator plagued him with doubt and concern.

But change was needed. There had to be a better way for the Werefolk to live. The divide between the Underkingdoms of Earth, the poor treatment of the widely considered "lesser" Werefolk to the Apex nations, and the bubbling discontent from Human leaders created a powder keg ready to explode. Who knew what spark could throw everything into chaos?

He had been told of the silent war Humans had waged against vampire covens in the not-so-distant past. Apparently, a few vampires were fool enough to author books about their existence and the existence of many covens of vampires. One particularly vain fool even became a rockstar of all things. Very public deaths at his final performance, and a supposed vampire "goddess" and the Humans were done with them. Their immortality and manipulation frightened the Human governments, provoking their leaders to eliminate the threat before it could consume them. Despite their supernatural abilities and immortal lives, the vampires had been systematically wiped out, their existence erased from history, surviving only in fictional stories and films. Legendary creatures are brought low by their arrogance and greed.

His musings were cut short by a second coughing signal from his left, indicating it was time to move in. He waited a few more minutes, observing the occasional flashlight of the mountain villa's exterior patrols wink out as his elite team methodically eliminated the guards. Then he stood and began walking towards the villa, remaining in the shadows but moving with the casual ease as if a man on a pleasant Sunday afternoon stroll.

As he neared the outermost ring of patrols, Dromon, one of his lieutenants, appeared beside him. "Milord, they are humans," Dromon whispered, his voice barely audible over the wind.

Luther said nothing, but his eyes sharpened with alertness. Why would she use humans for protection? Caution replaced eagerness as this odd factor raised suspicions.

"Everyone pull back! It's a trap!"

A scream of pain from his left told him his revelation had come too late. He and his team were in grave danger. The cunning adversary had outwitted them, and now they would have to fight for their lives to escape.

Hyde drew a deep breath, his resolve hardening. As he led his team into the fray, he couldn't help but wonder if this struggle was worth it if the path to peace and unity required such darkness. But there was no turning back now. The fate of the Pack hung in the balance, and he would do whatever it took to secure their future.

As the battle raged on, he knew that his actions would be judged by history. Whether he was remembered as a tyrant or a saviour would depend on the outcome of this night and the choices he made in the days to come. For now, all he could do was fight, survive, and hope that, in the end, his intentions would pave the way to a better world.